IRRESISTIBLE

ALIE GARNETT

12-153-44 PUBLISHING

For my M & G, for putting up with me.

CHAPTER 1

WATCHING Melanie walk out of the loan office was just the sign Mathias Nordskov had been waiting for. Not a good sign. If things were going his way, she would be shaking his hand and having him sign the papers with a smile. Based on how she couldn't make eye contact with him now, Melanie leaving meant she couldn't tell him no herself.

Math wasn't surprised. She had grown up just two miles from him and had been his sister Julia's best friend all through school. Math had watched her grow up, and now he was watching her walk quickly to her boss's office on the other side of the bank.

This was not the first time he'd been turned down for this loan, but this was the first time the loan officer hadn't turned him down right away. This was the third bank he had tried, and it was looking like a strikeout. They all said that his debt was too high at this time to buy more land. But he needed more land—he wouldn't be able to grow his farm without it.

Today he had dressed in his best gray slacks and a crisp white shirt with a tie in order to impress the banker, making it seem like he wouldn't have any trouble with a loan of this size. By the looks of it, he should have just worn his chore clothes.

Melanie had disappeared into the office across the bank, but she didn't come out of it. Instead, another woman came out. Coolly, she walked across the bank in her high heels, tailored knee-length black skirt with a matching jacket over a light gray shirt. Her ash blonde hair was pinned up on her head. She was not smiling as her eyes trained on him. Another bad sign.

Feeling trapped in Melanie's office, Math was well aware of the new bank president; she was notorious throughout the county for being difficult. The word around was that she was a witch, but with a capital B. Few people liked her, and fewer had gotten a loan in the last eighteen months that she had been there. That was why this bank hadn't been his first choice to get the loan ... it was his third.

Now she was walking right towards him to shoot him down. Trying not to squirm in his chair, he knew he should just get up and walk out of the bank. No, he would take all the money he had in the bank and then walk out. This had been his bank his entire life—who was this woman to tell him no?

"Mr. Nordskov, I am Tess Thorn. Melanie says that you are here about a loan?" Her voice was pleasant sounding, but she talked slower than he had expected, probably because she was gearing up to deliver the death blow.

"Ms. Thorn." Reluctantly he shook the hand she had offered. Her perfume filled the room with the smell of summer flowers. It almost made him smile. It was January in North Dakota, the time of year when the snow was so deep you forgot summer even existed.

Math knew bad news was coming when she closed the door behind her. Good news never came behind closed doors. It had been behind closed doors almost three years ago that his former wife said it was over.

"Mr. Nordskov, I have looked over your loan application, and I do not see that it would be in the bank's best interest to give you a loan today. If you had a twenty percent down payment, we would feel more comfortable with the loan. But for today, we are going to have to say no," she said politely.

Looking the woman up and down, he wondered how old she was.

She looked young, too young for her position. But the lines around her eyes said she was older than he thought. Those blue eyes looked at him. *No*, he decided, *they're a gray color, not blue at all.* The blazer covered most of her body in a boxy square. Her legs were long, and her heels made them longer. She had nice legs.

His perusal of her must have been too slow because she crossed her arms before asking, "Did you hear me, Mr. Nordskov?"

"I heard you, Ms. Thorn. You said no."

"I said not today."

"Tomorrow then?" He knew he sounded like an annoying kid, but he couldn't help it. She just rubbed him the wrong way.

"Most likely not." She shook her head.

"When?" he demanded.

"I do not have a date for you," she replied in her slow, clipped manner.

"You know I have banked here since I was six?"

"I saw that, Mr. Nordskov. But that does not change the fact that your debt ratio is too large right now."

"You're not from here. The moment you are gone, I will be back in here. And I guarantee that I will be getting the loan I want," he promised her.

"You're right; I am not from around here. And just so you know, if you do get someone to finance this loan and default, you will lose your farm. You know, the one that has been in your family for generations? Your grandkids won't get to live there. That is why I turned you down."

He watched her turn and walk out of the office. At the door, he thought she was going to turn around and say something else, but she didn't.

There was no reason to stay, so he jumped out of his seat and followed her out of the office. His eyes went to her butt, and he decided the nice sway was wasted on that woman. To her credit, she did not turn around as she walked to her office.

Walking out into the freezing cold January afternoon, he hurried to his pickup in the parking lot. Once inside, he sat in the cold, looking at the bank in front of him. It looked friendly, but looks could be deceiving.

The last year had been a bad one. He had been hemorrhaging money from new equipment and fixing old equipment. Math needed the loan to increase his acreage, which would increase his cash flow. This year was going to be an interesting one without adding the land he needed.

Glancing at the clock, he realized school was out. He needed to get the kids. Starting the pickup, he was glad he lived in a small town because he was only a few blocks from the school. It was the same one he had attended for twelve years, and now his kids were there. Cora was fifteen this year and would be graduating too soon for Math to think about. Mason was eleven, but he was so different from how Math had been at that age. He had a hard time connecting with his son since the divorce. The baby, Juniper was seven and probably in a class with Melanie's son or daughter.

Karen walking out on him had been a surprise. He hadn't even noticed that she was unhappy. Had he been unhappy too? Maybe, but marriage was supposed to be forever, whether there was happiness or not. Since they hadn't fought, he had assumed they were doing great. He had been wrong.

Just like he had been wrong to try and get a bank loan from that woman.

CHAPTER 2

WHAT WAS SHE EVEN THINKING? Tess Thorn thought to herself as she sat alone in a booth at Mia's café waiting. *Who was she even waiting for?* Ruth Kennedy, that was who. She worked as a secretary downtown at the insurance office. But who was she, really?

After a few hours of drinking alone at home days before, she had posted on Facebook to see if anyone had read the book about Ted Bundy that had just come out. Almost immediately, Ruth had responded that she had read it. Right away, Tess had messaged back about the book, and they chatted about what they each thought about it. That had lasted for a few hours. Once Ruth had asked to meet and actually talk in person about the book, Tess had jumped at the idea.

Now she was waiting for her fellow fan of murderers to arrive. Looking out the window, she watched as the wind picked up and blew snow down Main Street. It was starting to look like the storm was going to arrive early. At least her trip home was a short block away.

The door opened, which let in a blast of cold air, and a platinum blonde woman walked in whose hair was messed up by all the wind. Ruth Kennedy had arrived. Though they had not been introduced, Tess had seen the woman a few times since arriving in town, usually from a distance or across the bank. She watched as the woman took off her jacket and hung it up on the coat rack, then started her way.

Before she made it past the first booth, she stopped and talked to the two men in a booth closer to the door. Both had been there since Tess had arrived. She knew them by name, but not personally. One was Ruth's boss, and the other, it seemed, was not well-liked by the blonde. Watching the interaction, Tess felt like an outsider because she barely knew any of them, but they all looked like they'd known each other since forever.

Soon, Ruth was sliding into the booth across from her. A smile was on her pleasant face despite what had happened on her way to the table.

Tess stuck out her hand to her. "Tess Thorn."

Still smiling, Ruth took her hand and replied, "Ruth Kennedy."

Dropping hands, they looked at each other, neither knowing what to say. The tension was broken when the cafe's owner came to their table, dropped off two glasses of water already talking, "Here are the menus. Hey, Ruth, not at your mom's today?"

Tess didn't spend a lot of time at the cafe, so she didn't know Mia very well. As far as she could tell, Mia was very friendly and knew a lot of people.

Ruth's smile turned brittle as she turned to the waitress and replied, "Mia, no, it's storming, so I'm staying in town."

"I suppose.... Wouldn't want Chester to have to drive in snow." Mia said looking out the window.

"Mia," Ruth warned.

"Sorry, there's just a little tension in here right now," Mia stated, looking around the nearly full café. "You and Rafferty now, and Natalie Beckett and Hazel May are here. I don't think either one knows." Mia walked away. A few of the names were familiar to Tess, but not enough to make her feel a part of the conversation.

Tess watched as the waitress walked away. Turning back to Ruth, she asked, "You and Rafferty Brooks?"

She hadn't lived in town for very long when she had been introduced to Rafferty Brooks. Though he hadn't hit on her yet, he was known for flirting with most of the tellers when he came into the bank. Something Tess kept a close eye on.

"Not like that. Ick. He is just a jerk, always has been," Ruth assured her.

"You could do worse," Tess said with a shrug.

"*Ick*," Ruth emphasized her feelings for the man.

"So, what did you think of the book?" Tess asked, getting back on topic.

Ruth turned to look at her. "What did you think about it?"

"What book?" Mia was back with her pad for their orders.

"You wouldn't be interested," Ruth replied to the friendly waitress.

"The new one on Ted Bundy," Tess answered at the same time.

"I think the author had a major thing for him. It was kind of creepy," Mia said off-handedly as she tapped her pen against the notepad and watched customers enter the café.

"You read it?" Ruth sounded shocked as she looked at the waitress.

"I thought that too," Tess agreed at the same time.

"I read a different one a few years ago that was way better on him," Mia said after taking their orders before she was called away by another customer.

"Maybe we could invite her too. She has read more than one book on Ted Bundy, so she might be interested." Tess wanted to get more people involved—two people did not a book club make.

"No, not Mia," Ruth replied quickly.

"Why?" Tess asked as the woman in question slid their plates onto the table, silent this time.

When she was gone, Ruth whispered, "Mia is *Mia*."

"Maybe you guys could bond over serial killers and your dislike of Rafferty Brooks. Looks like she has no time for Mr. Flirty either," Tess said.

Across the café, Mia had grabbed his knit hat and threw it on the ground, just before she slammed his head into the frosty window. The woman said something only the men could hear before spinning and stomping back into the kitchen.

"I guess you can. But I'm not," Ruth said.

When Mia finally made it back to their table with their meals, Tess asked Mia if she was interested in joining a book club. The time and place were set by Mia herself. It would be tomorrow, right there in the café.

The time went by fast as they talked, and soon Mia had brought their bills to them. Just after she dropped them off, the door opened, letting in another blast of cold air and a small family. Tess was surprised to see Mathias Nordskov in the flesh again. It had only been a few days since she had turned him down.

Instead of the dress pants and a pressed shirt, he was now wearing a heavy green jacket and blue jeans, tight-fitting blue jeans. His blond hair was wind-blown, and he was trying to fix it but failing. She wanted to run her fingers through it herself to see if she could do any better.

She diverted her mind away from thoughts of touching him as he followed a teenage girl past her table. Two smaller children followed behind, one mid-sized boy and a small girl. Tess could tell that they were his children because they looked so much like him, blond hair and all. But she couldn't help but look for a wife or girlfriend. Though Tess saw no one, she figured there must be someone. No way was Mathias single.

As he passed by table after table nearly everyone in the place called a greeting, and every one of them called him Math and not Mathias. Even Mia, but Tess liked Mathias so much better for the man.

He walked past so quickly, and she wondered if he had even noticed her, not that she cared. She could still feel his anger at her for telling him no to his loan request, but the risk was too high for her even to consider it. Melanie had told her that morning that Mathias was coming in, and Melanie knew him too well to tell him no. Not wanting to ruin Melanie's relationship with the man, Tess had delivered the bad news instead. When he had lost his temper, she was glad it was geared towards her and not the younger woman. Melanie hadn't been a personal banker for long enough to be able to handle that much anger. Tess, on the other hand, had years of experience in that department.

Bills paid, she and Ruth both grabbed their jackets from the rack by the door. Both headed out the door and down the street into the blowing wind and snow. Ruth stopped at the insurance office. "This is me."

Tess laughed. "You are going to work?"

"No, I live above it," she admitted with a grin.

Tess pointed at the next building. "Then you are my neighbor. I live right here."

"Yes, we are," Ruth said, not sounding surprised.

"See you tomorrow then?" Tess asked, hopeful that the other woman would show up tomorrow, even if she wasn't overly happy that Mia had been invited.

"Yes, at three," Ruth answered.

In a few more steps, Tess entered the stairway to her apartment. Carefully, she walked up the steps—she often tripped on the narrow steps when she wore heels. Once on the landing, she unlocked her door and closed it behind her. After shrugging off her jacket and boots, she sat down on the couch, grabbed a blanket off the back, and snuggled in.

When she had moved in eighteen months ago, she immediately put the couch against the window. She loved to watch the world outside. She had spent many afternoons sitting right there, looking over the back of the couch at everything from rain to snow to just plain sunshine.

The best part of living downtown was that she only had a two-block walk to work. Within minutes of locking the bank, she could be home, changed and drinking wine. Or if the day was a bad one, something stronger.

Pulling out her phone, she looked through her texts. She had four waiting for her to respond to, but nothing important, so she set the phone back down.

Tomorrow she was getting together with two women from town to discuss books. Though she had read the book they were going to talk about a few weeks ago, she remembered it well enough to discuss it without reading it again. She was more nervous about getting to know the two women. In the eighteen months since she had moved there, she had found it hard to make friends. It had never dawned on her that you make most of your friends at work; however, people usually don't make friends with their boss.

This was the first bank she was president at, and she had worked for years to get to this point in her career. After getting her degree in finance, she worked as a financial advisor for a long time. Then over a year before, she had applied for a few presidency jobs and had landed the one in Landstad, North Dakota. She gladly took it. It was a small bank in a small town, but she hoped to use it to get a presidency job closer to where she grew up.

Though this was the farthest she had ever lived from her parents, she had yet to be within a few hours of New Paris, Minnesota. With a nine-hour drive between them, she had only made it home a handful of times in eighteen months. Her parents did not visit her … ever.

Leaning her head on the couch, she remembered the look on Mathias's face when she had said no to him. She knew he knew the answer already. He wasn't stupid, just frustrated, and he had taken that frustration out on her.

It had stung when he had pointed out that she was not from Landstad. It was true, but it still hurt. Fitting into Landstad had been the biggest challenge of her job, and she had failed. She knew she was an outsider, and everyone else knew it also. Even the bank employees didn't let her into their group. That hurt too.

Tess knew she had a reputation around town of being a strict, unbending, rule-following witch. But she had to be; she was a woman in charge. If she were a man, she would be called none of those names.

Until coming to this town, she had never been called any of those things. Well, maybe rule-follower, but she had been that way since birth. At her last job, she had been friends with everyone in the bank, and the bank was twice the size of the one in Landstad.

Tomorrow she would find out if she could still make friends. Maybe after thirty-five, making friends was not a possibility. Was that a secret that older women never talked about? That you can only have the friends you made in your twenties?

Pulling out her phone, she sent a text to her best friend, who was hundreds of miles away.

Tess: Have you made any friends in the last year?

Natasha was also thirty-six. They would have been friends since the day they had met. The conversation between them, together or apart, was ongoing. Natasha talked about her marriage and her kids and her hopes and her dreams. Tess only had her job and her hopes and dreams to share, but she had far fewer than her best friend.

Tasha: I don't think I have left the house in the last year.

With just a few words, Natasha made Tess laugh. Her mood lightened a little, thinking about her friend. It was hard to believe how close they still were. Natasha had gotten married at seventeen and now had eight kids between the ages of seventeen and one, and she had never had a job. Tess's life was her job, and she had never had a child or even come close to having one.

Tess: Tell Alex you need a date night.
    Tasha: I will not. That is how we got the last one. ;)
Tess: Worth it?
Tasha: She was worth it, but we maybe could have used a couple more years between the last two.
Tess: Last?
Tasha: Yes, last. No more.
Tess: Maybe one more? Or at least to an even ten?
Tasha: NOT TEN.

Tess laughed again. Tasha wanted two children but somehow got eight. She actually had a little excuse for every one of them. The first was an accident, but they were going to get married anyway. The second was okay because they were married. The third was a snowstorm, nothing to do. The fourth was because the first went to school, and she got lonely with just two at home. The fifth was their anniversary. The sixth was something about turning thirty. The seventh was because her husband got a new job, and the celebration went too far. And now the eighth was date night.

Even though Tess had not been happy when Tasha had given up her dreams of college and career to get married, she knew her friend was so happy with the life she had made. Probably happier than Tess was.

> **Tasha:** How did the book thing go?
>
> **Tess:** Good, we are getting together tomorrow afternoon.
>
> **Tasha:** Fun?
>
> **Tess:** Yes, fun. You never were interested in the dark side of humanity.
>
> **Tasha:** Nope. But you be you. Alex is home—got to pretend to be doing something.

She laughed again at her friend as she put the phone down. Most conversations ended with Alex since Alex is Tasha's world. Getting up, she grabbed a bottle of wine from the fridge and poured herself a big glass. Wine helped everything, unless the world got to be too much—then only vodka would help.

Tess had always wondered if she and Natasha would still be friends if they were not related. The family connection kept them close beyond the time when friendships usually fell apart. Natasha was Tess's step-niece, though she never actually thought of her as such. They had been friends more than relatives. It was just nice that they were both at family functions.

She sat back under her blanket and finally read through her other texts. Her sister, Ilya, sent some pictures of her new grandchild, a boy this time. Another nephew was raising money for a school trip. Natasha had sent a picture of her two little girls reading on the couch. No caption or message about it, just a picture. Her oldest brother sent a short message about coming home the next weekend.

Sighing, she responded to Mike that it was too far to drive for a short weekend and that maybe he should put it off until February. Really, she was lying. Until winter was over, she didn't drive over five hundred miles, knowing it could snow at any time. Her car did not handle snow well.

Mike sent the text every week, trying to bully her into coming home more often. Sometimes he mentioned their aging mother as if she didn't know that her mother was turning seventy-eight this year. Their mother hadn't had Tess until she was over forty, even older than Tess was now. But she was ready the next time he mentioned their mother since Mike himself turned sixty this year.

Looking out at the snow, she wondered what her mother had thought when she had told her twenty-three-year-old son she was pregnant. He'd already had three kids of his own at the time. In fact, Tess was born with nearly nine nieces and nephews. Four were her brother Alex's stepchildren, but that was never an issue in their family. Nor was it odd when his stepdaughter Natasha had married his nephew, Alex. It was just accepted as things that happen.

Ilya's text was expected. She had two children who were having babies this month. Ilya was just like Natasha, just a decade older. She'd been married forever, had a bunch of kids, and now had grandkids. What made Ilya different was that her first husband died in a car accident after fifteen years of marriage, leaving her with six small children. At the time, her sister had been only thirty-three. For two years she, was a single mom with a job and all the stress that involved. No other sibling had been unwed after the age of twenty except Tess.

That had come to an end when Ilya had fallen back in love with her high school flame, who was also widowed with seven kids. So together, they had thirteen kids, only to round the number to eighteen before they stopped having babies altogether. Ilya would be spending the rest of her life sending pictures of grandbabies to Tess.

Taking a notebook from the side table, Tess added the information for the new baby on the appropriate day. When she left home at eighteen, she had invested in a book to write down all family births and marriages. There were few dates that were empty. A few deaths were listed and only one divorce, but that was Tess's own failed marriage.

Being a part of such a large family made it hard to be away from them, but she loved being in the middle of the conversations, the yelling, the teasing. It made her own life seem quiet. But she was different; she had little in common with all of them. She had a four-year degree, whereas none of her five siblings had graduated from high school. She lived nine hours from home, and they each lived within three miles of her parents. They all had long marriages and had many kids; she had divorced after a short nine months.

Tess set her notebook down and picked up her tablet. Maybe she would read another book about Ted Bundy before tomorrow's meeting. She'd rather get lost in a book instead of dwelling on her failings.

CHAPTER 3

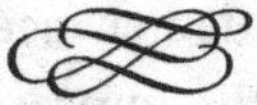

"Not what I heard. I heard you gave her a mouthful." Mia was scolding Math as if she had the right to tell him what and what not to do. Just because their mothers were sisters didn't give her the right to talk to him like that.

"I lost my temper," he explained. Somehow, his conversation with the bank president had gotten around town. It seemed the consensus was that he was in the wrong. But *they* were completely wrong. Including Mia Lawson

"Just be nice to her. She's having a hard time here." Again, she looked over at the blonde a few booths from them.

"She seems to be doing pretty well." He took the opportunity to look at her head and shoulders again. Today her hair was down and slightly curly, just reaching her shoulders. He liked this look better than the bank look. It was far more relaxed.

"She puts up a good front, but just leave her alone," Mia warned.

"Fine. Just get us burgers all around," he replied, stopping the conversation, which made the kids all change their orders before Mia bounced off to help someone else.

Looking at the back of her head again, he wondered what Mia was talking about. With her friends and a good job, she seemed like she was doing just fine. Just then, she got up, and he caught sight of her butt in tight-fitting jeans, maybe too tight since they fit like a second skin, making her rear look even better than the skirt had earlier in the week. And the purple sweater was shapelier than the blazer had been, giving him more of a hint at the curves below. Her figure was excellent for such a witch!

As she paid for her lunch, he saw her laugh at something Mia had said behind the register. It made her face light up and seemed to relax her, though she hadn't given the impression she was tense. Strangely, he thought he had heard her laugh, though it was across the crowded, loud room.

Math continued to watch as she put on her coat and left the restaurant. Since he was near a window, he was able to watch her walk down the sidewalk until she and her friend separated, and she went into a door near the pharmacy, maybe the door on the other side.

Hailey's voice brought him back. "Dad? Can I?"

"What?" He turned back to his oldest daughter, her face in the shape of a strange pout she had started using last summer. He still hated it.

"You weren't listening," she whined.

"What do you want?" He tried to stop thinking about the banker, but she was clouding his thoughts even when she wasn't here. Since seeing her he had been unable to wipe her from his mind.

"Beth asked if I could go over there. Can I go?"

"It's storming, Hailey," he reminded her.

"We're in town already. You can just leave me here."

As tempting as it was to have just two kids for a while, he knew he would have to come into town and get her later. Beth's parents wouldn't want to drive her to the farm. And if the storm turned into what everyone said it would, he didn't want to come back to town.

"No, Hailey, maybe next weekend," he replied as the food came. But he was sure that wouldn't work either because it was his ex's weekend. He'd make her be the bad guy for once.

Nobody said anything as they ate, but Cora sent him faces every few minutes, faces that said her life was awful and that she hated him. Nothing new.

Mia's words came floating back into his mind. Was Tess really having trouble settling in? It had been almost two years since she came to town. But he remembered the look in her eye when he had said she wasn't from here; was that look pain? Had his comment hurt the unfeeling bank president?

CHAPTER 4

LISTENING to Mike rant and rave at her was one thing; it was normal. Having him do it when the temperatures were hovering at thirty below zero when Tess was not wearing a coat was too much. Her brother was getting on her last nerve.

"Mike, I refuse to talk to you about this right now. I have things going on." She listened as he made snide comments about how he would have her married if he had his way—same old ramblings.

"You have no control over my life anymore!" she yelled into the phone as she shivered a little. She was only wearing a leather jacket, but the wind was cutting through every piece of clothing she wore.

Before her brother could make a comment, she lowered her voice a little and added, "You sure do have a way of ruining someone's birthday."

His immediate defense was to say he didn't know it was her birthday, and that was probably true—birthdays got lost when there's one every day in the family. She didn't actually think he knew when her birthday was; she couldn't tell you when his was. Maybe in June?

She ended the call without waiting for him to comment. Leaning against the cold wall, she took a few deep breaths. It was always hard talking to her brother. He didn't respect her but somehow needed her approval. Talking to him in public was twice as hard since her brother only spoke to her in Russian. So, her conversation with him had been him speaking Russian and her speaking in English.

For years she did not speak Russian outside of her apartment. Even though it was her mother tongue, and she could speak and write it, she only used it with her family. Her mother wouldn't learn English. Though she could understand it, she would not speak it to this day. Her dad could converse in both languages. Since all her siblings had managed to marry fellow recently emigrated Russians, they all knew the language. Her family, too, had emigrated to the United States when she was eight.

Russian was still the language she used when she got mad. Usually, she only got that mad at her family, so it didn't matter. During her short marriage, her husband had said it was annoying to be yelled at in another language. During high school and college, she had focused on clearing up her accent, and now most people didn't even realize she was not a native speaker.

Pushing away from the wall, she finally went into the bar. Mia had texted her a few minutes ago and asked if she wanted to drink. At the time, she had agreed so she could see her new friends. The bonus was that she could spend her birthday with others. But after her call from Mike, she needed a drink more than anything else.

Shoving the door open, she felt the warmth of the bar engulf her. She looked around for her friends, flexing her fingers to get the feeling back in them. With a quick glance, she needn't have worried, because the place was dead.

Mia yelled from a booth, "Dress down, lady! You're making us all look bad."

Tess laughed at the waitress. She was fun and outgoing, something that had taken getting used to. Stopping at the bar, she ordered a glass of wine and looked over at her friends.

After a few weeks they were friends now. The Sunday afternoon meeting had turned into a biweekly get-together. They had also changed the idea of the club a little the first day by having everyone read a different book, and then they'd compare them. And now they were going to start recording their conversations because Natalie said they were too funny not to share. It was weird, but Tess was going with it to see what happened.

"Should we call the younger ones?" Mia scooted over to let Tess sit next to her with her wine. The other book club members were in their early twenties, and Mia liked to point out their youth.

"No, Hazel has the baby, and Natalie should be with her fiancé today," Ruth said.

"How about Mandy?" Tess asked the two, even if Mia had been the only one speaking so far. But then again, Ruth was usually more reserved than Mia.

"She is in Grand Forks for the weekend," Mia explained.

"So, everyone had a bad day?" Tess asked the little group.

"You got that right." Ruth was staring daggers at the men at the bar. Tess hadn't noticed them when she came in. Not that she would have noticed them anyway; she didn't know a lot of people from town. To her, one pair of strangers were no different than another pair.

When Ruth turned back to them, she said, "What? It was Rafferty Brooks who killed my day."

"He always seems harmless to me." Tess sipped her wine and glanced at the two men again. She didn't know them well at all.

"Has he turned his smooth moves on you? He likes to bang anything in a skirt." Mia downed her shot of whiskey, then slammed her hand to her mouth. "No offense, Tess. Your skirts are always nice."

Tess just laughed at the purple-haired woman beside her. "No, Mia, I have not had the attention of Mr. Brooks. I think I am a little too old for him anyway." Tess felt old today. Maybe because it was her birthday, and she was now thirty-seven. Soon she would be forty, and then what? Fifty? Sixty?

"Too old? That has never been an issue with that one." Mia waved to the bartender for another drink.

"Then I think I am going to have hurt feelings since he has yet to pursue me." Tess looked over the man in question again. He was definitely younger than her, close to Mia and Ruth's ages, but he was a handsome man with that brown hair.

"Don't. You don't want to waste your time with him," Ruth said, shaking her head. "Anyway, he has a thing for Mia right now."

Mia's gaze flew to Rafferty. "He can keep his thing to himself."

"So, there is a hot man who has a job and his own hair, and you don't want anything to do with him, Mia. Why?" Tess asked the waitress.

"Because the minute I get enough money together, I'm out of this town. I'm a big city girl trapped in this dinky town, and Rafferty would only mess that up. Besides, he's a player," Mia pointed out.

"I would play with that if it were looking at me that way." Tess laughed at Mia's expression. She loved that her new friends could take a little teasing.

Paul, the bartender, brought over drinks for the table and indicated that they had been paid for by the guys. Once he left, Mia leaned into the table and whispered, "I tapped that once. Not going back."

"What?" Ruth asked in shock. "Paul?"

"No, Rafferty. A long time ago, ancient history now. But still a history not worth repeating." Mia downed her new glass of whiskey.

Ruth turned her attention to Tess. "So, how old are you, anyway?"

Tess looked over to her trying to hide her surprise. Did she know it was her birthday today? How could she have possibly figured that out? "How old are you, Ruth?"

Mia jumped in with the answer, "She turns thirty-one pretty soon, sometime in late winter if I remember right. My birthdays in the summer, and I will be twenty-nine. I need to be out of this town by thirty."

Tess looked over at the woman. "I will never get over how much you know about people in this town. Do you know everybody's age here at the bar?"

Mia's eyes scanned the room at the dozen or so people in the bar. Looking back at Tess, she answered, "All but you. I'm sorry, I'm a people person."

"That is what makes me say you can never leave this town. It will fall apart." Tess waved at the bartender again.

"I know. I can't imagine the café without Mia yelling at someone for something. Never going to be the same," Ruth agreed with Tess.

One of the guys from the bar brought the drinks over, handed them out, and said, "Peace offering from Rafferty and me." He only had eyes for Ruth as he said it.

Looking him up and down, Tess analyzed him from his shiny black shoes to his dark hair. He was good-looking too. From the time she had spent with her new friends, she knew he was Ruth's boss, Anderson Miles. She didn't know him at all, since he didn't have any money in her bank, "It is going to take more than a few drinks to put yourselves right with these ladies. More drinks and one of those little cardboard pizzas might help."

Anderson laughed. "Coming right up, ladies."

Ruth watched him with longing as he went back to the bar, then she turned to the women. Both were watching her, and she demanded, "What?"

"You have the hots for your boss," Mia stated in a loud whisper.

"I do not," Ruth defended herself.

"Oh, she does. He is a fine one, too. Should I head out and leave you guys to them?" Tess asked.

"No!" both women said at the same time, and all three broke out laughing.

The conversation turned to Mia and Ruth gossiping about a building that had recently changed hands in town. Tess couldn't figure out the significance of the conversation, but both women were very into it.

From beside her, Mia said, "I can't drink these. I'm already buzzed."

Turning to her friend, she grabbed the still-full wine glass in front of her and put it in front of Mia, swapping Mia's whiskeys for the wine. Tess drank them, one after another. It felt good going down and banished the thought of getting old from her mind. She added the empty glasses to the pile in front of Mia with a satisfying clink.

"I am never having a drinking contest with you." Mia's brown eyes were wide in amazement.

"Drink your wine, you lightweight," Tess said with a laugh. It actually surprised her that most people couldn't drink as much as she could. Maybe it was that her family was big on social drinking, and they socialized a lot. Tess had her first taste of Vodka at her sister's wedding when she was ten. She had been limited to three that night, but nobody had actually kept track. She smiled at the memory of Natasha and her drunk in the back of the reception hall at ten years old.

"I could have drunk them; I just shouldn't. I have to walk home after this. You know the rules about drinking and walking. Friends don't let friends walk home drunk." Mia laughed. Tess knew she lived across the street from her, just over a block away.

At her words, Tess smiled as she got up and went to the bar, leaning on it to get the bartender's attention. She then heard a voice beside her.

"You're still in town, Thorn?"

Turning, she saw old blue-eyes himself—and not Frank Sinatra. Mathias Nordskov was drinking at the bar. How long had he been there? She hadn't noticed him at all, though her back would have been to him as she sat with her friends.

"Mr. Nordskov," was all she said, not daring to call him by his first name, though she wanted to say it out loud. Just once again.

"Just waiting for you to leave town." His eyes swept her body from head to boot, lingering a little too long on her breasts. She wanted to hate it, but couldn't seem to not be a little flattered.

"Well, you have a long wait in front of you. I have no plans to leave," she replied, happy to see Paul finally coming her way.

"What can I get you, Tess?" Paul asked with a friendly smile, so different from the man beside her.

"Mia said she needs more alcohol. So, two whiskeys and one of what he is having." She pointed at Mathias.

"I wouldn't take a drink from you if you had the last alcohol in town. When are you leaving again? You don't really belong here," Mathias hissed quietly, so only she heard his words.

Not letting him see his words affect her, she asked Paul for two more whiskeys. Paul had them filled and then made a mixed drink and set it in front of Mathias. Tess handed the bartender her credit card and turned to Mathias. "Since you do not want this…." She drank the liquor, not reacting to the fizz of the pop or the burning of the whiskey in it. She just drank it like water. Silently she thanked the dozens of weddings and family events she had attended over the years.

Paul gave her back her card, and she took the whiskeys to the table. After setting them on the table, she slid into the booth again. "Sorry I drank your whiskeys, Mia. I got you extra as a peace offering."

Mia's eyes were as big as saucers looking at the four full glasses. Taking one, she drank almost all of it before setting it down. "Bluff called, Tess. I'm a lightweight."

Tess and Ruth laughed at Mia's defeat. Tess had known the woman would in no way finish the alcohol, but she needed another drink herself, especially after her talk with Mathias. Somehow, his words always seemed to bother her more than anybody else.

Tess took the glasses from in front of Mia and quickly drank the three full ones, then finished the one Mia hadn't finished and added the empty glasses to the pile in front of Mia. The burn helped drown her emotions, and the buzz was a nice side effect.

Just as the pizza showed up, Tess decided she had had enough of bar night, and she had hit her limit. The pizza looked like cardboard, anyway. With goodbyes to all, she headed out of the bar.

It was fun getting together with friends, but Mathias had turned the night sour. His anger was getting to her, and she had no idea why he was having such an effect on her.

But she didn't like it.

CHAPTER 5

Drunk, Math decided. *She was drunk.* He had been watching her all night, flirting with Rafferty Brooks and Anderson Miles. She and her friends. They had been buying the women drinks since he came in just before her. Tess, in her fancy leather jacket and skin-tight jeans. Tess with her hair all loose and wavy, sexier looking than she should have in a place like the Landing. *A bar was no place for sexy hair!*

Forcing himself not to look at her, all he could hear was her voice. Laughing and chatting about nothing, just loud enough so that he heard her every word, every chuckle. She was having a good time drinking fancy wine.

At first, he thought the ladies were together to celebrate Tess Thorn's birthday. When he had walked by her outside, he had overheard her talking with her ex about being controlled and that he wrecked her birthday. But nobody at the table had said anything about her birthday. Ruth had asked her how old she was, but Tess deflected the question. They didn't even know it was her birthday.

At his spot at the bar, he watched her drink Mia's whiskeys as if she were drinking water. When she had come to the bar, he had let his temper get the better of him again. He had been rewarded by seeing pain flash through her eyes before she could tamp it down. Sadly, he had found a way under her skin, and he had used it.

Karen had taken the kids for the weekend on a mini-vacation. His kids weren't even in the county tonight. They were hours away, having fun without him—which was why he had gone to the bar to see if something was happening. He wanted to get his mind off his failure as a husband. But instead, the bar had been dead, and he had just drunk alone, just like if he had stayed at home.

Tess had extended a peace offering, but he had rejected it. When she had drunk it, he saw the ice from the glass had left her top lip wet, and he really wanted to lick the liquid off it. She had very kissable lips for such an unlikeable person.

Once she made her way back to her table, he watched her drink nearly all the alcohol she had carried over to her friends. *She had to be drunk*, he decided. *Nobody drinks like that, especially no woman with great curves.*

Paul started to talk to him about football, and he stopped looking at her. Or tried to. When Paul was called away to get more drinks, he glanced back at the table, and Tess was gone. When had she left? Had she gone to the bathroom? He finished his drink, and she never came back out. She had gone home.

She was alone on her birthday, alone and maybe fall-down drunk on one of the coldest nights of the year. Why didn't her friends make sure she got home okay? She'd be alone and sad, all because he said she didn't belong there. He felt like a jerk.

"Damn it." He waved Paul over and paid for his tab, deciding to add a bottle of wine to go. Landstad may not have any fast-food restaurants or fancy liquor stores, but you could get alcohol to go from the Landing six days a week. Sundays were dry there.

Zipping his coat as he stepped out into the bitter cold, he walked across the street and down a block to the door he presumed led to her apartment. Math opened the door to a hallway that was only steps to a second floor. Checking the mailboxes by the door, he saw she lived in apartment A, whatever that meant.

At the top of the stairs, he spotted the A on a door and headed that way. He softly knocked on the door and waited. Suddenly, he realized he had no idea what he was going to say to her. What was he even doing here? This was crazy; he didn't even like her.

The door opened, and he saw she had changed. She was wearing an oversized pale green T-shirt and possibly shorts underneath, but Math couldn't tell. All he could see was bare feet and long legs. *Good god, they were long.*

Her phone was to her ear, and he heard her mumble, "I will call you back, Tash."

Her gray eyes were boring into him, and it was making him uncomfortable. Holding up the wine, he said, "Happy birthday."

"What do you want, Mathias?" Everyone had always called him Math, but he liked her saying his full name. Maybe too much.

"I brought you a gift for your birthday." He lifted the bottle into the air and smiled, hoping he would soon figure out exactly why he was there himself.

"Who told you it was my birthday?" She set the phone on a table by the door. He heard a text come in as she asked the question.

"You did." Another text sounded from her phone.

"I really do not think so." She crossed her arms over her chest.

"I heard you tell your ex on the phone that he was ruining your birthday." His eyes traveled south, and he noticed the fabric of her shirt was pulled tight across her ample breasts. She was most definitely braless based on the nipples peeking at him.

"My ex?" she asked, and he knew she had caught him looking at her chest because her arms unfolded and fell to her sides.

"The guy trying to control you. I assumed it was an ex." He heard another text come in, but she didn't seem to notice.

"I still have no idea what you are talking about." Her eyes were on his, making him not look back at her breasts.

"I heard you on the phone outside the bar."

"Oh, with Mike, you mean."

"I guess; I didn't catch his name," he admitted. He wasn't in the mood to talk about some guy who had once been important to the woman in front of him now.

"Why are you here?" she asked again, still holding his gaze.

He held out the bottle to her again. "I brought you a present."

She looked at it, and he glanced at her breasts again. Her eyes flicked back to his, and she caught him again. Without looking down, she took the bottle from his hand and put it on the table next to her phone, which had just received another text. She was popular, but then again, it was her birthday.

"Are you going to answer your texts?" he asked, half hoping she would so he could just leave. Except the last thing he wanted to do was leave now.

"They can wait. Thank you for the wine." Though she gave him a small smile, her face held the same expression it did when she had turned him down for the loan: controlled.

It was that control that annoyed him the most. He wanted to see the real her, not some mask that she had for everyone.

"I also wanted to make sure you made it home safe. You drank quite a bit." He noticed her eyes were not as glazed over as he had expected. She was soberer than he was.

"I am here, safe." She leaned against the door jam. Was this some sort of staring contest? If so, she was definitely winning because he couldn't keep looking into those eyes when there was so much of her he wanted to see.

The only positive was that she was not looking anywhere but his eyes. There was a part of his body that made it obvious that he liked what he was seeing. There was no way of hiding that from her if she happened to look down.

"I see that," was all he could think to say as he broke eye contact. She had scrubbed the make-up off her face, but her lips were still pink, still kissable.

"What do you want?" she asked, and her tongue came out and licked her bottom lip.

"Fuck it." Giving up on finding an innocent reason to be there, he leaned forward and kissed her. Her reaction was to freeze for a moment, but then she gave in to the pressure of his lips on hers.

Those soft, kissable lips were even better than he had imagined, better than he could dream. She tasted of whiskey and wine and something purely Tess, though he hadn't thought he knew what that tasted like. But he was sure that was it.

Stepping closer, he leaned his entire body into her as she returned his kiss. When his tongue slipped out to touch hers, her mouth opened and accepted it without hesitation. Math gently backed her around the corner of the doorframe until she was in the apartment, reaching over to shut the door to the hallway. There may only be a few apartments there, but he didn't need anyone to be nosy.

With her back still against the door frame, he braced himself against the wall with one hand and slid the other down her back until he could cup her ass in his hands—her perfect firm ass.

Tess kept kissing him as she slid open the zipper on his coat, then eased the coat off his shoulders. He dropped her ass so that the coat fell to the floor. This time, his hands slid under the green shirt, and he realized he was wrong—she wasn't wearing short shorts, just silky panties that were barely enough to cover her amazing ass. His hand went further up her hot, smooth back, confirming she didn't have a bra on either.

As their kiss deepened, he was unable to stop himself as he moved to gather her breasts in his hands. Feeling the smooth flesh, he had been eyeing for so long, in his hands made him groan in her mouth. They were just as perfect as he had imagined, big enough to overflow his large hands. The pads of his rough thumbs passed over her already taut nipples, and he felt her moan in his mouth.

He was enjoying himself as he caressed her breasts, and she unbuttoned his shirt, but not quickly enough for her, it seemed, because the last few she just ripped open, sending buttons flying. After pulling the shirt free of his pants, she skimmed her hands slowly up his stomach and chest to his shoulders. Once there, she eased the shirt off his shoulders and let it fall to the floor with his help. It landed on his jacket. Then her hands went down his back, but she raked her fingernails lightly down his skin, causing goosebumps to form all over his body.

If she could take off his shirt, Math was damn sure taking off hers.

Grabbing the hem, he pulled the green T-shirt over her head and tossed it on the floor on top of his. Pulling his mouth from hers, he gazed over her perfect perky breasts with their pink nipples. They were hard and pebbled from his touch. A series of shapes on her hip bone drew his attention for a moment. It was a small tattoo, and he would have to analyze it later. He had better things to do right then.

With his arms wrapped around her waist, he lifted her body until he could get her nipple into his mouth without bending. Tess's squeal quickly melted into an achingly sexy groan. As he lightly bit and licked her breast, she ran her hands through his hair and then gripped it to keep his mouth where it was.

Slowly, he slid her body down his so that she could feel how much he wanted her, but once her mouth was close, he started kissing her hard. He needed to taste her again. Sliding his hand down her body again, he pushed her panties down as he went, and they silently fell to the floor. With one hand, he caressed her breast, and with the other, he explored her mound, hearing her breath catch as his fingers slid through her folds. She was already wet for him.

Breaking the kiss, he heard her whimper as he ran a single finger over her clit. While stroking her, he matched the rhythm with his tongue on her nipple until, with a groan, her head fell back and hit the wall, hard. Nearly unfazed, she begged him not to stop as her hands left his hair to feel the back of her head. She must have decided that there was no damage as she started to lower her arms, but his free hand caught them and held them above her head as his other hand slid two fingers into her folds as his thumb continued to rub circles.

When her head fell back again against the wall, not as hard this time, he felt her breath catch as an orgasm took over her body. He watched as her eyes glazed over, and she started to shake her head and moan. Then, to his utter amazement, she started mumbling words that were not even words, just sounds spun together in what sounded like words.

As her body relaxed against the wall, he kissed her again. He wanted to move this to her bedroom, or at least to the couch. But instead of moving, his tongue explored her mouth, and his hands tried to memorize her every curve. Slowly, her hands went to the waist-band of his pants. Her fingers brushed his bare skin as she unbuttoned and unzipped, then pushed his jeans and boxer briefs down enough to free his painful erection from its prison, letting him kick them off his feet.

Her eyes raked over his body, so he took the moment to get a full look at her as well. He wasn't one to compare, but his ex had nothing on the banker's body. Karen's dedication to dieting since Cora was born meant she had been far more angular than the woman in his arms right now. The extra curves gave him more to hold on to, which was something he realized he had missed in a woman all these years. At least that was ending now.

When her hand went around his hard-as-steel shaft, his mind stopped completely. She started stroking him with a tight grip, and he almost lost all the control he had left. It had been a long time since he had been with a woman and a lifetime since he was with a new one.

"Fuck," he said through clenched teeth, "I don't have a condom."

Without a word, she pulled away from the wall and walked naked across the apartment. She was so confident in her body, and it made him just stand and stare at her, not follow her like he should have to take them to the bedroom. Instead, he was mesmerized by her ass and by how her blonde hair brushed her delicate shoulders. He hadn't spent a moment kissing those shoulders, tasting them.

All too quickly, she returned with a condom packet in her hand and a smile on her lips. It was too late for him to move further into the apartment; his feet were stuck to the floor. As she drew close enough, he pulled her into his arms to kiss the smile off her lips, leaving her panting.

She smiled again and leaned away, holding the condom wrapper with her teeth as she took his erection in her hand again. He watched as she caressed it and ran her fingers up and down his length, then stroked him a few times before reaching up with one hand and ripping the packet open with her teeth. Then slowly, she unrolled it over him. Too slowly.

At that point, he had never wanted a woman more than this one;

he was shaking with it. Grabbing her around the waist, he lifted her, twirling until her back was pressed against the wall so he could take her nipple into his mouth once again. She was so perfect. He slowly lowered her down the wall until his erection was pressing into her hot center. Watching her gray eyes start to lazily close, he smiled when they popped open as he slid into her, and then they squeezed shut with a moan.

Her legs wrapped around him as he slowly slid in and out of her. Math watched her as he moved; her head was thrown back, and she was moaning with each thrust. But he wanted more than moans. He wanted her so hot that she couldn't make words again. He picked up his pace, and she matched his movements, and soon, her moaning became one long sound. Before he could think, she had picked up the pace even more and was writhing in his arms. Moans turned into guttural sounds that turned into the crazy sounds she made when she came.

As she went over the edge again, the feeling of her tightening around him shredded the last of his control, and he came at the same time. As he pumped into her and tensed, she clung to him and yelled his name, "*Mathias.*"

He held her there against the wall as they breathed heavily and enjoyed the moments after sex. Math rested his forehead against her shoulder and slid out of her as he set her down on her feet. Looking at them touch the ground, he realized her toes were painted green like her shirt, but not recently done. The tops were white, showing that her nails had grown since she had gotten them done.

On the table next to them, her phone sounded—another text came in. She seemed to get a lot of texts, maybe birthday wishes. Both he and Tess looked at the phone, but neither commented on it.

Turning to her, he saw her chin go into the air as she took a ragged breath. Looking away from him, she said, "You can show yourself out."

Math watched her walk across the small apartment into what he assumed was her bedroom and shut the door behind her with a slam. Cursing, he realized he had fucked up. But even now, he didn't know what to say. He had never done this before. He had been married to the first woman he slept with and hadn't ever picked up a woman at a bar or at her door, whichever this qualified as.

He knew he should go and knock on her door, but he didn't know what he would say if she opened it. They didn't get along before; why should this change anything? It didn't.

Slowly he started to dress, thinking maybe she would come out. She didn't. Her phone buzzed again, and he picked it up.

Nat: Call me, sweetie.

The text was from someone named Nat. *Well, Nat can have her*, he decided. When he was fully dressed, he didn't have any reason to stay, so he quietly left.

CHAPTER 6

YEARS AGO, Tess's dad and brother, Alexei, had taken her and Natasha to a livestock auction. Tess had been fascinated by the fast-talking auctioneer and all the animals she saw. As the day progressed, she watched animal after animal being sold after much bidding and excitement. At one point, a lonely baby lamb was brought out; her mom had not wanted her, and she was next to be bid on. To Tess's surprise, nobody bid on the little lamb…. Nobody wanted her. Tess cried until her dad bought that little lamb for her. For years she had loved the lamb that no one wanted until it was old and died in her arms.

Looking out over the audience at Mia's Red River Flood Fund Raising Auction, she wondered if there was anyone out there that would take pity and bid on her. She knew how that little lamb had felt that day, looking out over an audience that didn't seem interested in her.

Tess couldn't shake the nervous energy racing through her, cursing herself again for letting Mia sign her up for this. Minutes ago, she had watched Ned Williams, who did catering, walk out onto the stage. He had also volunteered to donate his time and abilities for a good cause. He, too, had been suckered in by Mia to do this.

Today was April first, and Mia had approached her three weeks before to see if she would be willing to offer herself up for auction—well, her financial abilities, really. But in reality, the bidder could use her for almost anything. At the time, it had sounded a little fun, but today it sounded like hell.

Since Ned was popular in the community, a bidding war started. His price kept rising until, in the end the MC had asked the caterer if he was willing to do both parties for the highest bid, doubling the amount of money raised. Of course, he said yes; it was for a good cause.

This auction took place every year at this time, just before the river flooded with the snowmelt. Every year, the river swelled for hundreds of miles along its banks, causing all kinds of damage. Since Landstad was only a few miles from the river, there was always some damage, but this was the first year they were bidding off people and their talents to help the cause. Mostly it was just stuff, but this year, Mia had an idea on how to improve it.

So far, everyone who volunteered had made more than any one item had. Well, until Tess. She was sure there would be no offers for her.

Tess had plastered a fake smile on her face as she stood on the bright stage of the high school gym. It was so bright, she saw everyone's faces, which was not making this any better.

Before she could back out completely, Natalie introduced her, "Next, we have financial advice from Tess Thorn. She is the president of Landstad Bank. She has over ten years of financial planning and personal banking under her belt. Your bid on her will give you six full hours of her undivided attention. If you're not interested in organizing your money, she's also a mean cook, can run a vacuum, and argue you under the table."

Tess stopped listening and concentrated on not tripping. She had worn her favorite shoes, but sometimes the heels had a mind of their own. *Walk, do not trip.*

As the bidding started, Tess tried not to look out over the audience or listen to what was happening. She tried not to think about that lamb that only she loved enough to buy. The crack of the gavel falling caused her to look at Natalie for any indication as to what happened. Natalie was smiling at her and pointing as she said, "Math Nordskov is the highest bidder at $2,000."

Tess almost tripped. *What the hell? Two grand and Mathias?* Which was the bigger shock? She wasn't worth two grand, though she didn't know how much she would actually be worth. Ned hadn't even brought in two grand.

Wheeling around she rushed backstage without falling on her face.

Once backstage, Mia came up from nowhere and hugged her. "See?! I knew you would bring in some cash. And now you owe me two grand."

Tess had promised Mia she would match the funds that were raised when she was auctioned off. She never expected to go so high. "I will, uh, get you a check next week," she said as Mia hurried off, still grinning.

Mathias. Tess hadn't even seen him in the last two months. After what had happened, she had worked at avoiding him, but she hadn't needed to worry as she never ran into him at all. It was just wham-bam, and he was gone.

But what a wham-bam it was. Sadly, her insides tingled for hours after he had gone. If he had pounded on her bedroom door to be let in that night, she would have let him gladly, even if it had nearly broken her when he had nothing to say after it was over. But looking back, she knew she should have said something. At the time, she couldn't think until she had shut the door to her room. Then she had come up with a few ideas. But by then, he was already gone.

As she walked to the science room, she wondered why he would bid on her. Was it to yell at her for hours on end? Was it to criticize her? Both? Was it to have his wicked way with her again? God, she hoped it was the last one.

Entering the room, she saw he was already there, talking to Hazel May, another book club member, who was taking payments from the bidders. Hazel must have told him that she was there because he looked over his shoulder at her. He was not smiling as their eyes met; his had a cold glint to them.

"Mathias."

"Thorn."

"When do you want to do this?" She bristled at his use of her last name. He must have forgotten about the sex they had because he didn't seem to like her much again.

"When are you available?" His eyes went straight to her chest as he spoke, so maybe he didn't completely forget.

"Just give me a date. I can make anything work." Lifting her chin, she tried to sound professional, but it was hard with his eyes not meeting hers or even trying to.

"Tuesday?" His tongue darted out and ran over his upper lip ever so slowly.

"This one or next?" Her body went right to the memory of his hot tongue her breasts, and they started to tingle and ache.

"Next." He looked up with his blue eyes, dark with desire. He was thinking about it also.

"Where?" Her eyes locked on to his, and she folded her arms, trying to get her body under control.

"My place. Do you know where it is?" he asked, but it sounded more like a challenge.

"I can get the address from work. See you at eight next Tuesday." Tess turned on her heel and walked away from him. Tuesday was going to be a long day.

CHAPTER 7

TUESDAY DAWNED, sunny and slightly chilly. Since the kids were in town with Karen, Math was alone all morning, no breakfasts before the busy hustle of the day. Nothing to distract him from his thoughts, just him wondering what he had been thinking last week. Why did he buy Tess Thorn at the auction?

No matter how many times he asked the question, he knew the answer: because she looked scared and vulnerable up there on the stage. He didn't think others saw her that way, but he had read the look in her eyes. When Rafferty Brooks had started bidding on her time, he had to jump in to save her. Rafferty was a playboy in this little town. No way was he letting Rafferty spend a day with Tess. Math had assumed Rafferty was aware he wouldn't win, but he didn't stop bidding.

So, Math kept bidding as well to keep her away from Rafferty. It was only after he won that he realized *he* would have to spend a day with her. After he had paid, he saw her, and all he could think about was how much he wanted her again. God, he wanted her in his bed. The look in her gray eyes said she wanted to be there as well. But instead of actually talking to her and being civil, he had let his anger at the loan make him mad again. What was it about that woman that stopped him from getting over that moment with her?

So here he was, waiting for her to spend the next six hours with him. Over the last few days, he had come up with a plan to get her out of his system, proving to them both what a city girl she was. Once he saw how much she disapproved of farm life, he would be over her. Math had spent thirteen years married to a woman who had grown up in town and had no interest in the farm she lived on. Karen had done nothing but complain about every aspect of country life for their entire marriage. He was not making that mistake again.

A dust cloud on the gravel road he lived on announced her arrival. He looked at his watch, smiling. She was prompt. Math leaned against the porch railing as he watched her drive his way. He wondered what cute little luxury SUV she was driving, BMW or Mercedes most likely.

Her vehicle slowed and turned on to his bumpy driveway. He hadn't had time to fix it since the frost had let go, and there were large potholes down the entire thing. So, she drove with caution and swerved around the big ones.

The little red two-door Chevrolet had to be at least ten years old, maybe older. It looked to be in good shape, but it was not what he had expected her to be driving. When it stopped by the garage, she jumped out and petted Jonesy, his dog, acting like she did it every day. The dog's excited welcome was not what Math wanted.

Today she was wearing her tight jeans and an orange Landstad Tigers sweatshirt. How she made a sweatshirt look stylish, he didn't know. Smiling, he saw that she had pared the outfit with a pair of strappy sandals that had heels a few inches tall. Perfect for the day ahead.

Looking around, she gave him a smile. "Nice place. You grew up here, right?"

"Yes," he answered, but since she had gone into the back seat of her car to pull out a leather bag and coat, she was flashing her butt his way. Not that he was going to complain about the view.

She shut the door with her backside because her arms held a

computer bag and another bag that contained … he didn't know what. She turned to him, "Where to?"

"Well, first, we will put this stuff in the house, then get you some proper footwear." He led her to the house, letting her carry all her stuff. After all, she was here to work for him, so he was doing nothing to help her.

"I have sneakers," she replied from behind him as she followed.

"Sneakers?" he questioned. He had rarely heard that word describe shoes.

"Tennis shoes, then."

"You'll need a little more than that, Tess. It's spring. It's muddy out here." He opened the door and held it open for her to enter. As she passed by him, he could smell the summer flowers that she usually smelled like. Just the smell brought him back to her apartment so many months ago.

"Can I just set my things here?" She gestured to a bench.

"Yes. Try these on; they're Hailey's." He picked up and handed her a pair of rubber boots that had been discarded by his teenager the last time she had been forced to help him.

"Okay," she said and dug in her bag to pull out a pair of socks. It seemed she was prepared for more than computer work today.

Math leaned against the wall and watched her carefully take off her sandals and slip on the socks, then pull on a boot. "You will have to thank Cora for letting me use her Wellies."

"Wellies?" he asked with a raised eyebrow, still leaning against the wall watching her. Again, she looked sexy, just changing shoes.

"Boots. Rubber boots. Wellies?" She didn't understand his confusion.

"Just rubber boots around here. No fancy name brand," he replied, pushing himself off the wall. "Grab your coat."

Math left the house without looking to see if she was following. In a way, he was excited to knock her off her high horse with a little hard work and dirt. He led her to the calves' barn, where he had a load of small hay bales waiting. Her steps were slow as she looked around the yard.

"I need these piled up in this shed right here." He pointed to the spot. "I'll leave you to it."

He walked away without any further explanation. *Let's see how she does*, he thought to himself with a quiet chuckle. He knew he would spend a few hours rearranging the bales tomorrow or the entire trailer if she left right now. With her busy, he went over to the shed and started fixing an issue with his tractor. It had been having issues last fall, and sitting all winter hadn't fixed it.

After an hour of working on the tractor, he headed back to see how far she'd gotten with the bales. As he drew closer, he saw her standing on the top of the wagon, tossing a bale off, then another, then another. Agilely, she jumped down to the ground and picked up one of the bales, then carried it easily across the shed to the location he had indicated. She added it to the perfect stack of bales she had already put there.

On her way back to the ones she had on the ground, she saw him. He expected anger, but she only asked, "What is this building?" and picked up another bale.

"Calf shed. Calves can come in here but not the moms, so I can give them extra food without their mom eating it all." He leaned against the trailer and watched her carry the bale.

"Never heard of it, but I can see why it would be of use. I did not know you have cows." He walked back for the last bale.

"Yes, a few dozen black Angus. Do you know much about beef cows?"

"No, not about beef cows," she replied as she climbed back on the trailer.

Looking up, he noticed she was close to done with her first task in just over an hour. Once the bales started to fall, he helped her. Apparently, this hadn't been enough to have her running for the hills.

"Do they have babies yet?" she asked from the trailer.

"I'm in the middle of calving season right now." He stacked a bale.

Shoving another over the side, she said, "When we get done, can I see one?"

"A baby cow?"

"They are called calves, Mathias. You should know that." She laughed at herself and dropped another bale.

"Really, Thorn?" He couldn't help but laugh at her joke, mostly because she was so proud of herself for it.

"Yup." She jumped off the trailer now that it was empty.

Taking another bale from the pile of only half a dozen, he watched her grab one also and carry it to the pile. Then he saw she wasn't wearing gloves. He had forgotten to give her gloves in his hurry to get away from her before. Her hands must be killing her. The baling twine would have dug deep into her tender hands.

"Damn it." He dropped the bale he was carrying, pulled off his gloves, and grabbed her hands.

"What are you doing?" she asked as she let him inspect her hands.

"I forgot to give you gloves." Her hands were red where the twine dug into her skin, but so far, she wasn't bleeding. Carefully, he put his large gloves on her much smaller hands.

"I do not need gloves. I am fine," she argued, instantly starting to take off the gloves.

"From now on, you will be wearing gloves. I'm not going to be to blame if you get damaged."

"I am not really a glove person, Mathias," she insisted.

Turning, she grabbed the last bale and put it on the pile. Then she pulled off the gloves and tucked them into her back pocket. "What's next?"

Damn, she looked cute in her borrowed rubber boots. The chilly air and exertion had turned her cheeks red, and the wind had messed up her hair. It took effort not to pull her into his arms and show her what a good old fashion roll in the hay was. Almost more effort than Math had.

Instantly angry he turned, he walked away from her without saying a word, why was he thinking about her that way again. This time he knew she was following because he could hear her footsteps on the ground behind him. For a moment, he wondered what she was thinking, then dismissed it. She was probably thinking about leaving here.

"This next project was the reason for the boots," he answered, leading her across the yard to the old barn. It was dim inside the building. Over winter, he had to keep some cows in here for a few weeks. Her task was to clean the barn of all the hay, straw, and manure with a pitchfork and shovel. He already had the manure spreader at the end of the barn waiting to be filled—by hand.

"I need this clean," was all he said before walking away. Again, he left her to do it the way she thought it should be done. He would give her points for moving a few dozen hay bales, but this was going to take her some time.

This time he forced himself to stay away until lunch. He had ended up helping with the hay bales, but he told himself he wouldn't help this time. This time, it was all her. That had given him enough time to fix his tractor and get it put back together.

Walking back to the barn, he glanced towards the house, expecting her car to be gone. Half the time he had purchased was gone, and she hadn't said anything about finances.

Stepping into the barn, he saw her leaning against the wall of one of the old horse stalls. She had taken off her coat and wasn't wearing the gloves—they were sitting on her jacket, lying on top of a fence rail. But the pitchfork was resting against her body with her arm over it to hold it in place while she typed with her thumbs. Tess also had head-phones in, and he could hear the hum of music coming from the white buds in her ears. Her head was gently moving with the music.

She still hadn't noticed him when she slid the phone back in her pocket and started to pick up the pile of hay, straw, and manure she had created. Then she deftly carried it over to the spreader and threw it over the side.

Suddenly, she saw him standing there. Stopping, she pulled the headphones from her ears. "You are back."

"You're not wearing the gloves."

"I am not moving bales. No gloves needed for these tools." She pointed at them.

Stepping further into the barn, he saw that she was over halfway done with the project. Her efficiency amazed him.

"You still need gloves." He couldn't believe she had been working for over two hours with no gloves on again. Stomping over to her, he picked up her hands. He softly rubbed his thumbs over the red welts. Her hands were redder than they were before. This morning they had been white and soft, and now they were angry red but still small and warm in his big hands.

She pulled her hands from his. "I do not need gloves. I am fine."

"It's lunchtime." Math turned away from her and walked to the house, suddenly missing her hands in his. Although this time he made sure she was following, even if she seemed far more interested in the farm around her than him looking at her. Smiling at her stubbornness, he was starting to rethink his plan. Quitting wasn't in her vocabulary, and she would hurt herself before she admitted defeat.

In the house, he started to make hotdogs and a can of baked beans. As he poured the beans into a pot on the stove, he wondered if she was a vegetarian or something. But he decided she would probably rather eat meat than admit to him she didn't.

He heard the door slam behind him as she entered the house. Math wanted to look and see if she was okay, but he stayed in the kitchen. It took some time, but she finally came into the kitchen and set her leather bag on the table.

"Where is a restroom?" She was looking around the room for a clue.

He pointed down the hallway, and she headed that way. Once she was gone, he took out two plates and set them on the counter. Then he went to the fridge and took out ketchup, mustard, and two cans of pop.

She came back and was now carrying her sweatshirt over her arm. Under it, she had worn a Landstad Tiger's T-shirt. The shirt followed her curves like his hands had two months before, and he itched to do again.

"You have a beautiful home, Mathias. Very farmhouse, which of course it is." She was looking around his house. The large kitchen behind him had a big island in the middle. The dining room was nearby and held a large table and half a dozen chairs. He didn't even think she had seen the living room. His home didn't have a modern, open plan but was more broken up into smaller rooms.

"Thank you."

She put her sweatshirt on her leather bag. "Anything I can do to help?"

"No, I've got it." He loaded up their plates without asking how much she wanted. Then he slid them across the island to where the stools were.

Taking a seat in front of one of the plates, she reached over to almost the other side of the island and grabbed a pop he had set there. In the process, he was able to catch sight of her taut stomach as her shirt rode up. Sitting down beside her, he nearly reached out and touched her bare skin.

"You do not want any financial advice, I am guessing," she stated as she took a small bite of beans.

"Nope."

"Why did you bid on me then, and why that high?" She took another small bite of beans.

He told her the truth. "Because Rafferty Brooks was bidding on you. I didn't think you wanted him to win."

"I do not mind Rafferty, but I do not know him well. Mia and Ruth have big problems with him. I do not know why yet." She took a small bite of the hotdog, which she oddly cut with her knife before eating it with her fork.

"You never know what he would want from you," he warned.

"You mean he might not want to work me into the ground?" She winked at him.

"Yes, he might have wanted financial advice," Math replied in fake disgust, making her smile.

"I am good at finances, you know. I know what I am talking about." She cut her hotdog again.

"You want something on your hotdog? Ketchup, mustard?"

"No, this is good."

"It's better with mustard."

She shrugged. "It might be."

"Have you never had a hotdog with mustard on it?"

"Of course, I have, at some point. I just do not eat a lot of hotdogs."

"I can tell. You're supposed to hold it, not cut it up." He pointed at her plate.

"It is neater to eat like this." Tess looked at the hotdog on her plate.

"Here, take a bite. See how much better it can be." He held out his hotdog for her.

"No, that is okay." She cut into her hotdog again.

"Come on, Thorn. Eat it like a regular person, not a princess," he pressed.

"I do not eat like a princess," she defended

"Really? Tiny bites and cutting up your hotdog. Princess eating."

"Fine," she said and bit into the hotdog he still held out to her.

"How was it?" he asked. He loved that she was almost laughing as she chewed.

Swallowing, she answered, "It was fine. The same. I do not think I like mustard."

"How un-American of you," he said as he smiled and laughed.

She turned back to look at her plate and took another small bite of beans. They ate in silence for a while. At one point, he thought that she was going to pick up her own hotdog but then didn't and once again cut it up.

The silence was getting to him, far more than to her because she wasn't saying anything. Usually, he didn't mind, but he wanted to know more about this woman. "How many siblings do you have?"

"Five, all older than me. You?" She took the last bite of hotdog.

"Three sisters. Mandy is older, and the other two are younger. Six of you?" Pushing his empty plate away from him, he wondered what being one of six would have been like. Busy.

"Yes, I never think about it, though. Mostly I think that I only have a sister. The boys are different. They are older and were gone." She took a sip of her pop.

"That's how I feel about Julia. She is six years younger than me. I feel like she was little forever, and then suddenly, she was an adult."

She nodded. "Yes, kind of like that. All my siblings were married before I turned ten."

"Are you going to see them for Easter?" It was the coming weekend.

"Yes, I will head down there. I will be off that Monday to get back."

"Where are they?"

"New Paris," she said as if everyone had heard of it.

"Never heard of it."

"Down my Rochester."

"Minnesota?" he questioned. That wasn't even close to here.

"Yes, it takes around nine hours to get there." She took another sip of pop.

"How often do you see them?"

"Not often. I try to get there once a quarter, but some winters are bad, and in the summer, my employees need time off, so I have to work most Mondays and Fridays. Then I go earlier in the fall," she explained, but he knew things like that wouldn't keep him from going home, far more often than that if he didn't live within ten miles of most of his family.

"When did you see them last?" he asked, realizing he had seen his parents just a few days before on Sunday.

She tapped her lips with her fork before answering, "Christmas was on a Wednesday, so traveling was out this year. I think mid-October I took two days off and went."

"Not Thanksgiving?"

"No, the bank was open on Friday, and it is not a holiday my family celebrates." She looked at her plate as if she was embarrassed to even admit it.

"We all have our quirks." He tried to make her feel better about being different.

Whether it worked or not, she looked up and smiled as she set her fork down. "So where do Nordskov's come from? Norway or Sweden? Seems like everyone here is from one or the other."

It was true; there isn't as much diversity in town. "Denmark. I am about seventy-five percent Danish with a dash of English to round me out. Thorn must be English. Tess, the English princess."

She laughed at his joke. "Most likely. I do not know where it is from."

He was surprised that she wasn't even curious about it. "Haven't you ever wanted to ask?"

"No. It is the only thing I kept after the divorce. Just his last name." She shrugged. "It wasn't important when we were married, and since then, I haven't put much thought into it.

"How long have you been divorced?" He didn't see her failing at anything, much less marriage.

"Fifteen years this year. We were only married nine months."

"Divorce stinks."

"How long for you?"

"Almost two years, three since she left."

"Her choice, I am assuming."

"Yup. I thought it was going okay." He really didn't want to talk about this with her, mostly because he didn't want to talk about it with anyone.

"Just, okay?"

"Maybe we had some issues, but we never talked about it." He had wondered if that had been the problem. Had it been over, and he hadn't even realized it?

"I think it is getting heavy in here. You must have work for me to do." She got up off the stool.

Leaving the dishes on the counter, they got their boots on, and Tess pulled her sweatshirt back over her head, covering her tight T-shirt. He missed it already.

Once outside, he asked, "Did you want to continue in the barn or go with me to check for new calves?"

Her gray eyes lit up. "Do you even have to ask? Calves."

"Let's go then," he replied and grabbed her hand, heading towards the back of the house where the cow pen was. He slowed his steps to match hers as they went, though he didn't let go of her hand. He couldn't even force himself to.

Once they were in view, she started to ask about the cows. Nothing in general about them, but specifics about certain cows—how old is that one, does that one have a name, does that one get along with another one? He had expected her to be a little frightened about the large animals. When people who have never been around them get close to them, the person usually gets nervous, but not Tess. At one point, she walked up to one and petted its head until the cow wandered off.

How many days would it take for her to lose her excitement over the black creatures, to be uninterested in them at all like Karen?

Walking back to the yard after no babies were found, he thought she was a little disappointed. After making sure she had gloves on, he left her in the barn again. She went willingly.

After two hours, he went to check on her again, finding her sweeping the barn floor. He stopped her—sweeping was a little too much for the barn floor. But it was cleaner than even he would have left it.

His next project for her was a dirty one. A few weeks ago, he had removed all the grain from one of his steel bins, but it needed to be swept and cleaned of the remaining grain. It was a dusty and dirty job, perfect for the prissy bank president to end her day.

After opening the door, he leaned into the cavernous steel circle. She did the same, looking to see what he was seeing. Their shoulders were touching as he said, "I need this cleaned. All the grain goes into those pails, and it needs to be swept after you're done."

He looked over at her and thought that she was going to say something but held back.

Soon she asked, "Can I say no?"

"You still owe me two hours." Looking at his watch, he knew he had found something that was too dirty for her, too hard. This was what it was going to take to make her run.

"Anything else you can have me do?" She continued to look in the bin and started chewing on her lip.

"Scared?" He almost let her off the hook, almost.

"No, wheat dust makes me break out in hives." She sneezed twice as she said it.

"I think you can do it. You can clean up some grain, can't you? Or is this too hard after spending too much time in an office?" he taunted her as she backed away from the open door.

"Then I can leave?" She was looking into the bin still, just a few more steps from it.

"Yup, then you are done." He hated the disappointment he felt; he'd had a fun day with her.

As he watched her stare into the bin, he really wanted to tell her she didn't need to do this, but she had nearly run from the task. This was the one that would show him she wasn't someone he should waste his time with. After her performance all day, he had been able to see her here. He thought she'd enjoy being here, thrive here, but that wasn't what this day was about. He needed to be reminded that she didn't thrive here. She didn't belong.

CHAPTER 8

Tess looked around the bin full of grain and its evil dust. The sun was shining into the bin, and she could see the dust spinning in the air around her. The storage container was bigger than anything her dad or brothers had by a lot. Everything on Mathias's farm was bigger and newer than she was used to.

She sighed as she pulled the gloves back on, knowing they would slow her down, but her hands would be swollen to twice their size tomorrow if she didn't wear them. After pulling the top of her sweatshirt over her lower face and tightening the hood over her hair, she hoped it would be enough but knew it wouldn't be. Nothing ever was.

By the time she was twelve, her father had stopped making her help with wheat at all. It occasionally made her sick enough to be hospitalized, and he didn't have the time or money for that. She should just leave, but she wouldn't give Mathias the satisfaction of seeing her leave with work unfinished.

Already sneezing before she even started, her eyes were watering within minutes of stepping into the bin, and her cough started before she was half done. Her chest and arms were on fire from the itchiness of the hives that she knew were there. By the time she started sweeping the last of the kernels up, she knew she would be calling in sick the next day, and maybe the day after that as well.

As she put the filled pails in the grass alongside the broom and shovel, she wanted to lay down and catch her breath in the dustless air, but she knew she had to get home and showered. Pulling off her sweatshirt to get some of the dust off her, she laid it on a chair outside the house. She pulled off the borrowed boots but left her socks on, then grabbed her bags and left the house. Halfway to the car, she realized she had not put on shoes. She was still in her stockings. But she didn't care and was not going back.

Getting into the car, she leaned back on the seat and knew the hives were forming on her back too. They must be everywhere. Starting the car, she saw that it was only 3:45 pm. It had taken her around forty-five minutes to get the job done.

Driving as fast as she could, she got to town in half the time it had taken to get out to the farm. Relief washed through her as she found a parking spot in front of her door. After dragging herself out of the car, she quickly ran back to it to grab her computer—she was not coming down later for it.

She pulled off all her clothes outside her apartment door and left them in the hallway as she walked naked into her apartment and to her bathroom. She didn't wait until the hot water started; she just climbed into the cold shower and shivered. As soon as she was soaked, she realized she had to take her medicine. Without drying off, she climbed out of the shower and took the pills that would help, then climbed back into the shower and stayed until the warm water ran out. But then the cold water felt good, so she stayed for another few minutes until her teeth were chattering.

She didn't dry off. No matter how soft the towel was, it would just irritate the hives. Tess climbed into bed and texted her VP at the bank that she was taking two days off. Something she never did. Setting a timer on her phone for forty-eight hours she plugged it in, and let her medication put her to sleep. Maybe she should have just walked away from the wheat bin. She would have looked bad, but at least she would be alive.

* * *

HER TIMER WASN'T GOING off, so Tess knew she hadn't missed work, but who was pounding on her door? If her memory was correct, she had gotten up four times for more pills, bathroom breaks, and a little to eat. Then back to bed.

Every time she was up, she looked a little better, but not good yet. Her face was actually clearing up fastest, so she might be able to work soon. But not today. Picking up her phone, she saw that it was only Thursday.

The pounding came again. Tess groaned and dragged herself out of bed, pulling on sweatpants and a sweatshirt as she went. She wished she could just be naked. It was more comfortable than clothes. She wondered if she could take more pills when whoever this was left. She decided she would.

Pulling the door open, she saw Mathias standing with his hand in position to pound on her door again. He looked her over and demanded, "Where have you been? I stopped at the bank to drop off your clothes, and they said you've been gone for three days."

"Here," she mumbled. Her mouth was really dry.

"Do you know your clothes are in the hallway?" He pointed to the pile she hadn't done anything with, nor had her neighbor.

"Did you wash the sweatshirt?" She didn't reach for the folded shirt in his arms. He also had her sandals on top of the shirt.

"Yes."

"It can come in then." She took the clothes from him and turned to get a glass of water. Her throat was dry too.

"Are you okay?" He had followed her to the kitchen.

"No." She filled a glass with water, then looked at it in confusion. "Where did I get this?"

"Are you drunk?"

"I wish." She laughed. Maybe she should drink some wine instead, but she took a drink of the water and said, "This is not wine."

"Have you taken something?"

"Not enough. Tired." She ran her hands over her face. "What time is it?"

"2:40 pm." He looked at his watch.

"What day?"

"Thursday," he said as if she should know that.

"I have to call in tomorrow. Oh, wait, I have a timer. I will do it then." Smiling, she drank the water. She was tired, and she didn't know what he was doing there, didn't care. "I am going to bed."

Walking past him, she walked into her bedroom, stripping as she walked. No way was she sleeping in clothes; they rubbed everywhere. She dropped onto the bed on her stomach, then pulled the pillow under her head.

"Tess, what's wrong with your back?" Mathias asked from the doorway.

"Hives. Grain dust. Hives," she mumbled into her pillow.

"Why didn't you say something if it gives you hives?" he demanded.

"I did. You called me scared. I am not scared of anything." She let the chilly air roll over her heated skin.

The thoughts rolling through her mind were jumbled and confusing, but she just let them go. She only had a few hours left before the pills wore off again, and she might be normal. Might.

* * *

IT WAS dark and cold in her room when she surfaced again. Really cold, but the light from the living room was coming in the bedroom door. Rolling over, she cursed her lost days. Picking up her phone from the bedside table, she looked at the home screen and saw it was 8:00 pm on Thursday.

Cursing again, she saw that the timer she had set had not gone off. It should have gone off about two hours before, but it was silent. Next time she would have to come up with a better plan if the timer was going to fail her. Pushing the button, she saw she had thirty-three texts since she had taken the first pill. Most were from Natasha, thankfully.

Reading through them, she saw she had actually been high-texting Natasha most of the time. It was a good thing Natasha wasn't on pills that messed with her head … and that she didn't text anyone else.

Tess tossed the phone on her bed and rolled from her stomach to her back. Staring at the ceiling, she wondered if it had been a dream that Mathias had been there. Had it been a dream, or had she just thought he was there and had a conversation with air?

As she lay staring at the ceiling, trying to decide which had actually happened, she realized the blanket from the foot of the bed was laid across her cold body. Her cold, naked body. Her gazed snapped away from the ceiling to Mathias beside the bed. How long had he been there? Had she been naked the entire time?

"You're awake." He sat down on the bed beside her.

"How long have you been here?" She needed to know.

"Do you want water? Since 2:40 pm." He got up to get her water.

"No, I have to get up."

"No, you stay."

"*No*, I have to get up." She pulled herself out of bed and stumbled to the bathroom.

Once inside, she emptied her full bladder and washed her hands, wishing she had just a scrap of clothing in the bathroom. Even something dirty, but no, there was nothing. With a groan, she decided it was nothing he hadn't seen before; he had spent six hours in the apartment with her passed out naked on her bed.

Leaving the bathroom, she crawled back into the bed under the blanket he had laid on her. Math was no longer in the room, so she need not have worried. She could hear him in the kitchen. It was odd having someone in her apartment. She never actually had guests. Her apartment was small and was only supposed to be her home temporarily when she had moved to Landstad. But as the months went by, she just stayed, knowing she wasn't staying here forever. She did love how close it was to her work.

Math walked back into the room, carrying a glass of ice water.

Sitting up against her pillows, she took the glass from him and drank a little. It was cold and wet, and her body needed that right now.

"You did not have to stay."

He sat on the bed. "I caused this, so of course I stayed."

"I have dealt with it before. I know what to expect."

"Do you want more drugs?" He started to get up.

"No, I am over it, mostly. It usually starts to fade after forty-eight hours. Did you shut off my timer?" Maybe she could trust the timer as long as Mathias wasn't there.

"Yes, I didn't want it to wake you. You were in such a fitful sleep as it was."

"Side effect—sleepy with a hint of wakefulness. But worth the relief. Did I do or say anything odd or embarrassing?" She took another drink, a bigger one this time.

"No, just mumbled a lot. And you sent a lot of texts. I don't know who received those, but you kept them busy." He reached over her and grabbed her phone off the bed and put it on the nightstand.

"Tasha, my niece. I texted her as soon as I got home, so she knew what was coming." She looked at the phone.

"Why didn't you just tell me? I thought you were kidding." He touched her arm.

"You taunted me. It is my weakness. I will show you I can do what you think I cannot do." She set the now empty glass down on the nightstand by her phone. She snuggled further into the blankets because she was still naked. "Did you spend the entire six hours ogling my naked body?"

"Nope, I've been a gentleman," he said, but his eyes traveled to her breasts just under the blanket.

"You are no gentleman, Mathias. The hives make me hot, and fabric irritates it. That's why I am naked," she admitted as his eyes moved back to meet hers.

"I figured as much. They started to fade at four. You really had me worried." He ran a hand over her bare shoulder and then down her arm.

"No need to worry. I can take care of myself," she replied, lifting her chin. She had been taking care of herself for most of her life; she didn't need him.

"I got your shirt washed and went to the bank to drop it and your shoes off. The lady at the greeting desk thing said you hadn't been in most of the week and that you were sick. I had just seen you, and you were fine. Then you opened the door, and I thought I should be taking you to the hospital."

"Do not take me to the hospital. I have the meds already." She sat up a little—no need for a wasted trip to the doctor.

"And they make you so loopy I thought you were drunk." He was sitting far too close to her for her liking, or she liked it far too much.

"I do not get drunk."

"Yes, you do, Tess Thorn."

"No, I have not been drunk in years. I drink, but I do not get drunk anymore."

"You were drunk the night we, umm." His ears actually turned red.

"The night we had sex, Mathias. I was buzzed, not drunk."

His expression said he didn't believe her. "I watched you drink a crazy amount of alcohol."

"Nothing I could not handle, Mathias. I can handle my alcohol," she insisted, though it always sounded bad. Maybe it was better for him to think she was drunk.

"Sounds like a problem." He didn't even act like he believed her.

"Just a fact. Were you drunk that night?" She had known he was drinking but really didn't want it to just be a drunken hook-up.

He tried to change the subject. "I was buzzed, maybe just buzzed enough. Do you want more water?"

Watching him all nervous talking about sex and being drunk, she wanted to laugh at him but didn't. She didn't want to make him angry and leave. It was nice having him here. When he was friendly, she liked him a lot.

"What is your tattoo of? I admit I looked at it when you were sleeping. I saw it that night too, but I was thinking of other things."

Looking down at the spot under the blanket that would be her hip, she reached out with the hand he wasn't holding and touched it over the blanket. It had been there for years, and she barely noticed it anymore. It was just a part of her now.

"It is my maiden name in traditional Russian. I got it when my divorce came through, and I did not take the name back. I felt that I needed a reminder of who I actually am. Do not tell my parents; they will kill me," she said. The only one in her family who knew was Natasha, but she had never actually shown it to her.

He smirked. "Now it will probably be the first thing out of my mouth when I meet them. What does it say? I cannot read Russian."

"Aleksandrova. As in Son of Alexander, but the A at the end makes it '*daughter of*.' Thorn rolls off the tongue a little easier," she answered.

"Not your tongue. You make it sound sexy." He was looking at her mouth as he said it, making her wonder how she had said it that made just her name sound sexy.

"Thank you." On the nightstand, her phone went off.

"Take that. I will make you something to eat." He handed her the phone and left the room.

Looking at the phone, she saw it was her sister, Ilya. Answering it, she tried to remember to speak in English since her sister would mostly be speaking in Russian. Tess always had to remember that Ilya was sixteen when she had emigrated, not eight like Tess. It was harder for her to learn a new language. The two years they had spent in England waiting for visas didn't help her sister either. In greeting, she said, "Ilya."

"Terezilya, how are you?" her sister always called her by the name their mom had given her at birth, never the Americanized version Tess preferred.

"I am fine, just a small case of hives. I am over it now," she said to relieve her sister's worries. Natasha would have told on her, even from this far away. Ilya liked to mother hen Tess, and she usually let her. But sometimes it wasn't needed. Like now.

"Natasha told me. You should have called." Her sister sounded hurt.

"I am sorry; I was on the meds. You know they knock me out."

"How did you get into wheat dust?" Ilya accused her as if she did it on purpose.

"It was a mistake. I was helping a friend." Tess hadn't told her sister about the auction.

"You need to be more careful," Ilya replied as Mathias walked into the room and grabbed the water glass from her nightstand.

"Stop treating me like one of your kids," Tess said, watching Mathias's butt as he walked out of the room.

"When you act like one, I will treat you like one."

"I will hang up," she threatened, acting just like her sister said. Tess sat up straighter, changing the conversation since her sister would forever treat her like a child. "How is Papa?"

"Same, they are starting to act old,"

"I keep telling Mike they need to go to a care center. Mama cannot take care of him like she used to." It was the same argument she always had. Her brother never listened to her anyway.

"Mikhail would never put them in a home, Terezilya."

"Then he should move them in with him."

"He wants you to come home and live with them." Another old argument.

"I am aware of that, and I get an earful every few weeks about how the unwed daughter should be taking care of her parents." As if she didn't have an important job, as if Mike wasn't just a farm laborer.

"Are you coming home for Easter?" Ilya asked hopefully.

That made Tess smile. "Yes, do you have a room available?"

"No, we are full up this year." Ilya had too many kids to have a guest. Tess hadn't stayed with her in years, but Ilya still liked to be asked.

"I will stay with Tasha then." As she always did.

"You have more fun there anyway."

"We get on." Tess grinned, they more then got on, always had.

"I have to go. You call next time you are sick." She made Tess promise.

"You will be the first one I call when I start puking." Tess laughed at what her sister's expression probably was.

"Quit acting like a child," she scolded.

"Quit acting like a mother," Tess shot back.

"I *am* a mother," Ilya reminded her. Ilya was a mother over and over again.

"Love you, Ilya."

"Love you, Terezilya."

Hitting the end button, she just looked at her phone for a minute. Ilya had always treated her as her first baby. Her sister was eight years older than her, and from the beginning, she had treated Tess like her own. She had been there every day until Ilya married at eighteen, and Tess was ten. But she had only moved across the yard in those early days. Tess had been there for all her sister's early motherhood days. They had been very close despite the age difference.

Climbing out of bed, Tess grabbed a pair of panties and slipped them on before pulling on the sweatshirt and sweatpants again. No need to impress him since he saw her at her worse today. Any pretense at being sexy would be wasted now.

As she walked out of the bedroom, she ran her fingers through her hair, thinking maybe she should have tried with the hair a little.

"Are you hungry?" he asked as he was making a can of soup. He already had sandwiches on the table.

"Yes, thank you. You did not have to make me anything." She sat down at the table, realizing she hadn't eaten anything since they had shared lunch Tuesday afternoon. Now it seemed they were going to share another meal.

"I'm hungry, and you're probably hungry too. I'll make up something." He set out bowls and filled them with the soup. Setting the bowls on the table, he went back for the sandwiches and then again for the glasses of water.

"How was your phone call?" he asked as he finally sat down.

"Good, it was my sister." She took a small bite of the sandwich and put it down.

"That makes sense. I could hear your half of the conversation," he admitted.

"Sorry."

"She sounded worried about you." Mathias took a bite of his sandwich.

"She treats me like I am ten still most of the time." She stirred her soup but didn't take a bite.

He smiled at her. "Can I tell her about your tattoo?"

"No, she will give me her disappointed face and tell me I know better." She laughed and finally ate a spoonful of the soup. How was it better when he made it than when she did? It came from the same can.

"How much older is she than you?"

"Eight years. Mama said that when I was born, she put her doll in the closet and carried me around instead. So, she worries about me." She ate a few more small spoonfuls of soup.

"Sounds adorable. Cora was mad that Juniper was a girl; she wanted another brother. They are seven years apart." He continued to eat.

"The good part is that Cora might not get married at eighteen and start having kids right away. Maybe she will go to college."

He shook his head. "I can't imagine Cora having kids anytime soon. She can't even take care of herself."

"How old is she?"

"Fifteen."

"Is it as crazy as they say to have a teenager?" She knew so many teenagers but couldn't imagine having one of her own.

"Yes. She's constantly mad at me." He took a bite of his sandwich.

"She gets that from you." She smiled at him.

"That hurt, Thorn." He pressed his hands to his heart and leaned back like she had shot him.

Laughing, she said, "Sorry I did not give you that loan. I had my reasons."

Suddenly, she wished she hadn't said anything because he had lost his smile. "It's okay; I am working with a bank in Grand Forks. They seem to be more interested in loaning me money."

Pushing her half-eaten sandwich plate away from her, she said, "Please do not take it, Mathias. If you get a loan and have a few bad years, you could lose your farm. I am serious. I have looked at the numbers over and over again."

"The land is right next to mine. It's perfect," he argued, the smile now completely gone from his blue eyes.

"But the timing is not. Wait until you can put twenty percent down on it. Do not put a mortgage on the land you own. Rent for now. Then you could lose it all," she explained.

"I will not have a bad year," he insisted.

"Be serious. There are always bad years in farming. You just have to be able to weather them. This could take it all away from you, from your children." She stood up herself as she argued. He knew better. Why couldn't he just admit she was right?

"Well, with that, I will leave." He stormed over to the door and grabbed his jacket. After opening the door, he stopped and added, "If I want your advice, I will buy it. Oh, wait, I already did. Keep your nose out of my business."

She stayed at the table, watching the door for a long time, wishing she hadn't said anything. Wishing she hadn't reminded him who she was. They got along so well when he didn't remember who she was.

Finally, she got up but left the half-eaten food on the table. She was no longer hungry. Shutting off lights as she went through the apartment, she shed her clothes and climbed back into bed. She could do nothing but sleep off the remaining medication in her system and try not to think about Mathias Nordskov.

CHAPTER 9

EASTER SUNDAY PROMISED to be a warm one, and Math knew that soon he would be in the fields. But today was a day for church and then family time. This was his first Easter with the kids since his divorce. Last year, Karen had taken them.

Sadly, only Juniper was excited to attend the holiday services. Even he wasn't that into spending an hour in church. It hadn't helped that he had been in a bad mood since he had left Tess's apartment on Thursday.

Tess. Why hadn't he believed her when she'd said wheat gave her hives? Maybe because it sounded like such a bad excuse. But thinking back, why would she not want to do that task? She'd been willing to clean up cow poop and lift heavy hay bales. He should have realized that something was wrong when she had forgotten her shoes. What did she wear home if she'd left her shoes?

After he had purposely waited a day before bringing in her things, he had expected to see her all happy and healthy at work. Instead, she had been passed out in bed for almost three days before he found her. Alone. Because of him.

Finding her disoriented had actually scared him. At first, he had thought that she was blind drunk, but when she had passed out again, he found the bottle of pills in the bathroom. That's when he called his sister Mandy, who was a nurse practitioner. She had been happy to explain what hives were, that the pills were what she needed, but that they'd knock her out. There was nothing else he could do for her but wait.

Then sadly, she had teased him about being mean to the girl he liked, like a little kid. Which, looking back on it, is what had happened, except Tess had loved almost every minute of it, and so had he. He had liked talking to her and seeing her excitement over the little things.

He wanted to apologize to her, but he knew she had left to see her family for the weekend, and he didn't know her phone number. Oddly, he knew a lot about her but not her phone number. He knew Mia would have the number. Maybe he would ask for it after church that day. Then he could apologize for getting upset with her.

His loan had been approved, but he was now hesitating because of Tess. Was she right? Was he overextending in his rush to get bigger? Could he lose it all if the markets went bad? Was it possible that she was looking out for him and not just being a witch?

Math followed the kids into the church and to the pew his parents and sister Mandy were sitting in. He took his seat at the end of the row. His family had sat in the same pew every Sunday for years now. Mia's parents were in the pew in front of them, and behind them were a couple of teachers at the high school and their kids. Like every week.

Except Mia wasn't there. Math wondered if she was coming. If she didn't come, how was he going to get Tess's number?

Just as the service was starting and the minister walked to the front of the church, Mia snuck in with a friend. They sat down as quietly as they could in front of him. He knew that backside well. He had spent hours looking at it naked in her bed just three days before. Tess Thorn.

But she had told him she was going home for Easter. She'd even told her sister that same thing. Why was she in Landstad for Easter? Was it the hives? Had they not been better like she said it would?

Today she was wearing a white sundress with large red and gold flowers on it, and it had a back that dipped down to her bra line. Analyzing her back, he saw no signs of the angry red welts that had covered it, just smooth, soft white skin. Skin his fingers inched to touch again.

Why had she lied? She shouldn't be here now. Why was she here giggling with his cousin, Mia? Both turned and waved at his sister, Mandy, who waved back. How did Tess know his sister? This town was too small!

In the front, the minister started to pray, and he watched Mia nudge Tess and then lean over to say something and giggle quietly. Tess turned to her and put her finger to her lips in a shushing motion. Mia was worse than a kid in church, always had been.

After the prayer, the pastor asked everyone to greet those around them. Mia jumped to her feet and went to her parents to say hi, leaving Tess alone. She turned to see if there were any familiar faces, and she waved at someone behind Juniper, and Juniper waved back at her.

He saw the moment she saw him behind her. Not knowing what to do, he held out his hand, and she took it.

"Good morning, Tess."

"Mathias," she responded with a smile.

"I thought you were going home for Easter?" he questioned, still holding her hand, unable to let it go.

"I am."

Around them, people had started to sit back down, so he finally dropped her hand as Mia rushed back towards them. He hoped she hadn't noticed the handholding since she was a known gossip. He was sure she had missed it, but a glance at Mandy told him she had not. His sister might not be a gossip, but she missed little.

He studied her back throughout the service. What else was he supposed to do? During the songs, he watched her sway to the music and page through the hymnal, looking at all the songs. During the prayer, she read them from the book, and he watched as her finger followed along.

At some point, Juniper had moved up to sit between the two women. Math knew that his youngest daughter really liked to spend time with Mia. But now she was sitting next to Tess, who, since the pew was now full, had her arm running along the back of the pew and was twirling Juniper's blonde hair around her finger absentmindedly.

When the pastor announced the closing hymn, he heard her ask Mia if it was really over. Not like she was excited for it to be over, but amazed that it had taken so little time.

With the end of the service, the minister moved to the back of the church to greet everyone as they left. Tess got up following Mia as she bounced from her seat to leave. Ignoring Math as she did it, she was sure he was glowering at her without seeing it.

Mia greeted the pastor, who then turned to Tess with a smile. "Happy Easter."

"Not until next week, Pastor Ruston." She smiled at him, taking his hand in hers.

Math had always liked the pastor, that was until he touched Tess. Then he wasn't such a big fan. Not that he had any claim on Tess, but he had more of a claim than this man.

Ruston Abbott laughed at her answer, not pointing out that there is one Easter. "Eastern Orthodox, then?"

"Yes, it was a good service, but a little short for my taste. Barely worth getting ready for." She finally let go of his hand, and Math could breathe again.

"Next time you come, I could try and get another half hour in for you, but any more than that, and I will be fired." The pastor was still smiling when he shook Math's hand, though he had little to say to someone who wasn't a pretty woman, it seemed.

Moving on, the Pastor greeted his children, and everyone shuffled outside to the warm sunshine. He immediately spotted Tess talking with Mia, Mandy, the teacher's kid, and another blonde woman with a kid on her hip. His Juniper was standing in front of Tess, and Tess had her hands on the girl's shoulders like this happened every day. They were giggling about something. The younger women both said their goodbyes as their families left for Easter dinner.

"Are you ready to go, Juniper?" he asked his daughter.

"Can I ride with Mia?" she asked, still standing with Tess.

"I don't know if Mia is going," Math told his daughter, not asking his cousin the question.

"Yes, Math, dinner is at my mom's house. I'm going," Mia said sarcastically.

"I did not realize you would be there, Mathias." Tess crossed her arms, her hands leaving his daughter as if she just realized what she had been doing.

Mathias almost groaned at the movement since it pushed her breasts high and made him long to touch them again. Did she know and do it on purpose?

"Math's mom and my mom are sisters, so it's tradition," Mia explained to her friend, even as she gave Math the side-eye.

"I did not realize. I should just head home. I have things I should do before work tomorrow." She turned and started to walk away.

"Tess, I will make sure Math is nice," Mia started after her.

Mia finally caught up to her at her little red Chevrolet, and the two women talked for a bit before Tess got in her car and drove away. Mia stomped back towards him, no pretense that she was going to do anything but yell at him.

"What is your problem, Math Nordskov? I invited Tess to Dinner at my mom's house, and you made her feel like she wouldn't be welcomed." She poked his chest with her finger. Mia was nearly a foot shorter than him, but she had never backed down from a fight. She always stood her ground, even today.

"I didn't say anything," Math defended himself. It was true, but so much had already been said that he didn't have to.

"I thought after spending an entire day with her, you would realize how great she is." Mia poked him again.

"I don't know about great," he hedged, hoping Mia wouldn't see the truth.

"Because you are so mean to her. Do you know she matched your contribution to the flood fund? She told me before it happened that she would match the funds she brought in."

"So, the bank is out a little money." He smirked. It's easy to give away money that isn't yours.

"No, she did it, not the bank. She didn't give you a loan for a reason. I'm sure she has told you why," Mia said.

"She told me her reasoning, but it's not true," he argued.

"Why would she have it out for you? For what purpose?" Her words stumped him; he really didn't know why she would just be spiteful to him.

"Because she is an unfeeling witch," he replied.

"You keep thinking that, Math. But remember, she is home alone today—no family, no friends to spend the day with. Alone. Because of you."

"She was supposed to go home for the holiday, Mia."

"She is. Next weekend, when her religion celebrates Easter." She poked him again.

"There is only one Easter, Mia."

"Look it up, you idiot."

She turned and left him standing with his parents and two of his sisters looking on. Of course, one of them was Mandy, who was just smiling at him because now she knew who he had been with a few days before when he had called.

CHAPTER 10

Main Street in Landstad was dead. Tess knew it would be since everyone she knew who lived on the street would be celebrating with family today. That meant finding a parking spot right in front of her door was not a surprise. This morning, she had driven the four blocks to the church with the idea that she would have to drive to Mia's parents' farm, but now she just drove back home.

Heading up to her apartment, she tried to decide what to do with her day. Definitely read the book for book club. Though she had read this week's book already, she could get a jump on the next one. Or she could just get caught up on paperwork since she would be gone late the next week. So, nothing pressing.

Slipping out of her white sundress, she hung it in the closet for the next church service she would attend. It had been a little cold today in Landstad for the dress, but next weekend, she would get to spend at least three hours in a hot, stuffy church.

She sat on the couch with her leggings and oversized Landstad Tigers T-shirt, trying not to be mad at Mathias. But it was pretty hard since he had ruined the first holiday she had ever been invited to since moving to town.

Church had been far different than she was used to. Mostly

because it was in English, whereas she was used to hours of Russian. She and Mia had gotten looks from others for talking, but she was used to it. Pastor Abbott had been friendly and had only looked their way once.

Once again, the biggest downside of the service had been Mathias sitting behind her, staring at her. Why was it up to her to explain her religion to others? What did it matter that she was at his church? Only a few days ago, they had spent the entire day together and had seemed to get along. Now it seemed he was as mad at her as when she had turned down his loan.

Maybe this was a good day to call Tasha and just have a gab session. Though they would see each other next weekend, they never ran out of things to talk about.

Tasha answered on the second ring, "I thought you were going to a friend's for lunch?"

"I was, but Mathias was going to be there, which means I am home today." She tried not to let the disappointment show in her voice. After all, it was better to spend a few minutes with angry Mathias at church than spend the day at his aunt's house.

"You cannot let him push you around."

"It is his family."

"He owes you."

"He does not owe me. I chose to go into that bin." She decided to change the subject. It was bad enough that she couldn't get him off her mind. "What is happening there?"

That was always a great way for her niece to start telling all the gossip happening in the family, from births to fights to new jobs. As Tasha was telling her about her great-niece's wedding plans, there was a knock on Tess's door.

Getting up, she just let Tasha talk as she opened the door, expecting Mia or Mandy or both on the other side of the door. But when she saw Mathias, she shut the door on him and turned back to her conversation with Tasha. She didn't want to see that man again today.

Hearing the door bounce off something, she turned back to it.

Mathias's foot had caught the door, and it had bounced back open. He walked into the room like he owned the place as he shut the door behind him.

Taking a deep breath, she said to Tasha, "I have to go."

All she heard as she hung up was Tasha saying in excitement, "He's there, isn't he?"

She didn't answer as she put her hands on her hips. "Get out of here."

"I can't. I have to bring you to Easter dinner." He slammed the door closed, and this time it actually annoying latched.

Tess shook her head, standing her ground. "I am not going if you are there."

"I can't go if you *aren't* there." His eyes dipped to her chest, and she wished she had put a bra on when she had changed.

"Well, then, I guess you can just go home. I am not going." Crossing her arms, she tried to block her chest from view.

"I will drag you there if I have to." His nose flared, and his eyes didn't move.

"I would like to see you try!" she yelled back.

At her words, he stalked towards her, forcing her to take a few steps backward, even if he had no idea where she was going. There was no way she was letting him drag her to his aunt's house. It only took a few more steps before her back hit the wall, and he was still coming towards her. He stopped just inches from her, resting his hands on the wall on either side of her head.

"If you don't go with me to Easter dinner, I'm going to throw you in a grain bin and roll you around in wheat." He said in a low growl as his breath was hot against her ear, sending tingles down her spine, and heat spread through her entire body.

She narrowed her eyes at him. "You would not dare." Her hands went to push him away but couldn't get the energy up to move his body from hers.

"In a heartbeat, Thorn, in a heartbeat." His breath was on her neck.

"Do you really want to take care of me when I am sick again?" she said as her fingers fisted his shirt.

"I want to see you naked again." His lips touched her neck in light kisses.

"But I will be sick," she whispered as his lips traveled toward hers.

"Naked," he whispered as their lips met.

As his tongue plunged into her mouth, she pulled him closer to her, his shirt still clenched in her hands. This was madness, they were just yelling, and now they couldn't keep their hands off each other. Madness, but she wanted him so much.

With a growl, he pulled away just enough to trail hot kisses across her cheek and down her neck, and she felt his hand grab her butt. Cupping it, he lifted her until his lips were even with her breasts, the nipples straining against the soft fabric for his touch.

Tess held on to his solid shoulders as Math latched on to a nipple, fabric and all. Knowing she should stop and actually doing it were two different things, and at that moment, she had one goal. Wrapping her legs around him, she knew stopping wasn't going to happen.

Pulling away from the wall, Math carried her the few steps down the hallway into her bedroom, shifting his attention to the other nipple as he went. He sat down on the bed with her legs still wrapped around him. One last lick, and he lifted her shirt over her head, then tossed it behind him. Neither cared where it landed as he slid his hands into her stretchy leggings.

She worked at the buttons on his shirt, getting a few undone, then gave up and started working on his belt. Finding it easier, she unbuckled it and unbuttoned his pants before Math flipped her over onto her back. With proficiency she wished she possessed, he pulled her pants and panties off in one motion.

His voice was husky as he ran a finger over her tattoo. "You look so good without the red blotches."

"Mathias, please," she begged as she grabbed his shirt and bringing him back on top of her body, needing his body touching hers. Once there, she let go of his shirt and pushed his pants down his hips. Then she repeated the motion with his underwear, freeing his cock for her. Her fingers wrapped around it as he unbuttoned his shirt. His breathing hitched each time her fingers slid over the smooth skin.

With his shirt gone, she was able to enjoy the wall of muscle on display for her. That was until his fingers slid across her folds to circle her clit, then her eyes closed at the heady sensation racing through her body. His lips sucked her nipple into his hot, wet mouth, and she forgot everything around her but him.

She felt some shifting on the bed, but before she could open her eyes to see what Math was doing, his tongue had replaced his fingers, and she couldn't stop the scream of pleasure that came tearing through her. Tess didn't feel she was vocal in bed, but today she couldn't stop herself as his tongue, teeth, and lips made her hips rock as she came, until to even stop it from happening. Her usual control was completely gone with this man.

She let her fingers skate over the muscles of his back as he kissed his way up her body until she could grab his butt. His lips met hers as his tongue swept into her mouth.

"Tess, I don't have a condom!" he said, barely lifting his lips from hers.

"I am on the pill," she replied quickly, then added because she rarely just relied on that, "I can get one also."

"Perfect," he whispered throatily as the tip of his cock brushed against her entrance, just before he plunged deep into her, stretching her, filling her.

"Yes," she moaned as she matched his quick, hard thrusts. His fingers dug into her hips, making her world come apart at the seams. Before her body had a chance to stop throbbing, he growled low in his throat as an orgasm shot like lightning through him.

Spent, he slowly rested his forehead against hers, breathing heavy, his arms holding him up the only thing that kept him from crushing her. Lowing himself to drop a delicate kiss on her lips before, Math pushed himself off of her, and they lay side by side as their heartbeats returned to normal—if normal was possible with Mathias in her bed.

After a few minutes of silence, Mathias sighed and propped himself up on an elbow beside her. He looked down at her naked, sated body before running a hand over her bare hip. "You better get dressed. We have to get to my aunt's."

Tess sat up quickly, glaring at him as she desperately tried to find something to cover at least an inch of her naked body, suddenly embarrassed by what had happened. "What?"

Grinning, he bent down to kiss her bare shoulder. "Easter ham is waiting."

Then he was off the bed, gathering up his clothes, and pulling on his underwear.

"I am not going to Easter dinner with you, Mathias." She finally grabbed her pillow and put it in front of her body.

"Yes, you are." He lazily pulled up his pants, zipping and buttoning them slowly. He hadn't taken his eyes off her.

"No, I am not." Tess got up and walked across the room, watching him still sitting on the bed, pulling on his clothes.

Without a word, he grabbed the pillow and tossed it to the floor as he pulled her onto his lap and kissed her. She tried not to respond, but her body immediately returned the kiss. Math smiled against her lip, pulled back, and said, "Yes, you are."

She pushed off his lap. "You cannot use sex like that!"

"I'm not using sex." Letting her go, he stood up as well. "Sex just happened. I'll just drag you with me to dinner."

"I cannot go to a family function after just having sex with you," she replied with a huff, watching as he picked up her panties from the floor.

He handed her the panties on his finger. "Yes, you will."

Grabbing them from his hand, she cursed him under her breath in Russian.

"I assume you're saying something about how much you're looking forward to having Easter dinner with my family." He went to her closet and pulled out the white sundress she had worn to church.

"I do not think so, Mathias." Hopping on one foot for a moment, Tess hurried to put her panties on, not because he wanted her to but because she didn't want to be naked anymore.

Removing the dress from the hanger, he held it up and said, "If you don't go with me, I will just tell my mom and my aunt that you couldn't come to Easter dinner because you were too embarrassed after we had sex."

Her eyes widened. "You would not!"

"Yes, I would." He plopped the dress over her head with a sexy grin. *A damn sexy grin!*

"You are an awful person, Mathias."

"And you are beautiful in that dress, but your hair looks like you just had sex. You had better fix that." He waved his fingers at her head.

Turning to go into her bathroom, she mumbled to herself again in Russian. And not about how much she was going to enjoy dinner at his aunt's house. She would not give him the satisfaction.

By the time she felt she was presentable, and Mathias had ushered her out of her apartment, she had only been home for around forty-five minutes. So, when they drove up to his aunt and uncle's house, the meal wasn't even on the table. It was still around an hour from being ready.

When they walked through the door, Mathias announced to the women in the kitchen, "I brought her. Now leave me alone."

Tess watched him walk into a room full of men looking into a corner. *Must be the living room*, she thought. She turned toward the women in the kitchen who were all looking at her. "This is not awkward."

"See? I told you he would do it," Mandy said from a barstool at the island.

Until then, it hadn't dawned on Tess that Mandy and Mathias were siblings—they were like twins. Neither of them had said anything about it, and she hadn't put two and two together until that moment. For a moment, she wondered who else she knew in town was a part of this family, but dismissed the thought. She didn't know that many people in town.

"I owe you money, Mandy." Mia grinned from the kitchen with a woman who must be her mom, based on the similarities between the two.

Walking over to Mandy, she sat down next to her on the open stool. With everyone's eyes still on her, Tess hoped she didn't look like she had just had sex. Which only was in her head because Mathias had said it because she hadn't had sex hair when she had gone into the bathroom earlier. Which meant she didn't have it now. She touched her hair to make sure, just in case.

"How did he get you here?" Mandy asked with a knowing grin.

"A lot of yelling and some possible idol threats," Tess replied to her friend. She could tell everyone in the room was listening.

Mandy laughed. "That's how he gets me to do stuff too."

From the living room area, a woman rushed to the kitchen. "Math said he apologized, and that Tess is here."

"Mom, this is Tess." Mandy pointed at her. "Tess, this is my mom, Dolly."

Tess turned to the woman she could tell immediately who had given her children their looks. Holding out her hand, she said, "Hello, Mrs. Nordskov, I am Tess Thorn."

Dolly took her hand and laughed. "We aren't so formal around here; just call me Dolly. That's my sister, Dotty. You already know Mia, and my Kit is here somewhere."

"Mrs. Lawson, are your other girls here today?" Tess asked. Mia was one of six girls.

"Just Mia and Kipling; she's in the living room, sleeping. Call me Dotty." Tess knew that Kipling was the baby of Mia's family. The teenager wasn't immune to her sister's gossipy ways, after all. Everyone in town knew that Kipling and her longtime boyfriend were no more. The other four sisters lived in other towns around the area, and Mia didn't say much about them.

"So not everyone comes home for the holiday?" Tess asked the room. It seemed odd that everyone wasn't there, but then again, she wasn't always there for her family functions. Everyone else was, though.

"No. Those who can will, and those who can't. Well, they don't." Dolly laughed.

"Does your family all get together? Mia said you celebrate next weekend?" Dotty asked.

"Yes, it is next weekend, and I am the only one who lives a distance. But I have always been able to make it home for Easter."

Dolly smiled at Tess. "Where are you from?"

"New Paris, Minnesota," she answered as she saw Math walking into the kitchen to get a snack off the table.

"I've never heard of it," Dotty replied.

"It is down by Rochester," Tess stated.

Dotty's expression was a little surprised. "Oh, that's far."

"It is, but I am used to it."

A taller woman who looked a lot like Mandy came in carrying a baby. It seemed that all Nordskov's looked the same. "Can someone hold James? I have to deal with Josiah."

Kit's mom eagerly turned towards the baby, but Kit had already decided who would hold the baby before she had even asked. Kit walked over to her sister, Mandy, and tried to hand the baby off, but Mandy deflected. "Tess, you can hold him. I bet you don't get to hold babies all that often."

Tess only laughed and took the baby. Mandy obviously didn't want to. Tucking him into her arm, she looked at the blond baby with familiar features and laughed. "Do all Nordskov's look the exact same?"

"Yes, they do," Mia and Dotty said from the kitchen.

Tess grinned at their answer. "How old is James here?"

"Just over two months," Mandy replied. She was looking at the baby with a longing and sadness Tess had never seen from her friend before. Did that have something to do with why Mandy hadn't wanted to hold him?

Tess looked at Mandy. "That little?"

Math's daughter, Juniper, came running into the kitchen, stopping when she saw Tess had the baby. "Is that the baby?"

"Yes, it is, Juniper," Tess replied.

She climbed onto Mandy's lap to look at the baby. "His name is James. I can't remember his middle name."

"Lee," Dolly provided her granddaughter.

"Lee," Juniper repeated.

"What's your middle name, Juniper?" Before meeting the little girl, Tess had never heard that name before, which might be why she had instantly liked the girl. It wasn't because of who her father was.

"Madison." Juniper was still looking at the baby, who was still sleeping.

"Juniper Madison Nordskov?" she asked.

"Yup, what's your middle name, Tess?" The little girl looked up at her.

Smiling at the girl, she replied, "Alexandra Sophia." It was really Aleksandrina Zsophia, but Tess was not going to explain that today.

"That's beautiful," Dotty said.

"Thank you. I have always liked it."

"Mine is Marie." Mandy winked, directing her fake disappointment towards her mom.

"Next time, Mandy. I will do better next time," her mother said with a smile.

"So, how far are you from the cities in New Paris?" Mia asked.

"About two hours, I think," Tess replied, bouncing the baby since it was thinking about waking.

"You must get there all the time," Dotty said as she checked on the ham in the oven.

"No, I have never been." She watched the baby to make sure he'd gone back to sleep. Looking up, she saw all eyes on her.

"Never been? It's two hours away."

"Never had a reason to."

"Would you be opposed to me riding with you and going there next weekend?" Mia said in half jest.

"Sure, Mia, but remember it takes nine hours to get home. So, we would leave at six on Friday night and will get in around three on Saturday morning. You will have to sleep on the floor at my niece's house—I get the couch. And the kids get up before 6:00 am, after which I cannot promise you a ride to the cities," Tess said, and Mia was shaking her head in the negative already. "Oh, and with no ride, you will have to go to church with me. It will be at least three hours long, and some of it is in Latin."

"No, thank you. Enjoy your weekend," Mia replied, holding up her hands in defeat.

Tess laughed at her friend. She didn't mention that the rest was in Russian or that there would be eight children, none of which were quiet. Or that lately they usually had at least two friends over at once, making it even worse.

Movement behind her caught her attention as Math left the room. How long had he been standing there listening? Watching?

CHAPTER 11

MATH FOUND himself between Tess and his sister, Mandy, for the meal. Since there was not enough room around the table, his and Tess's chairs were touching. And so were their legs under the table. He quickly realized that Tess was a lefty, which made it nearly impossible to have any room to eat. On Tess's other side was Mia.

He looked over at his cousin, who had all the room in the world, and he was stuck bumping her elbow with every bite. How had he never realized Tess was left-handed? He had noticed everything else. *Her eyes are gray, her hair is ash blonde, she can't form words when she has an orgasm…. Everything important.*

After passing bowl after bowl and platter after platter, he noticed she was not taking a lot of food. Though she arranged it nicely, she didn't take much of anything. A little of everything, but very little.

"Why aren't you eating?" he whispered to her.

"I am." She gestured at the food on her fork.

"That's not enough," he whispered.

"Yes, it is," she hissed back.

Mandy looked over at him. "Quit fighting."

"We are not fighting," Math said to her.

"Yes, you are," Mia said from the other side of Tess.

Looking at the women beside him, he would have lost his appetite if it wasn't after one in the afternoon. Mandy was now talking to Kit, and Tess was whispering with Mia, leaving him nobody to talk to.

"So, Tess, how is the bank?" his dad called down the table at her.

She tore herself from her conversation with Mia. "Good, Mr. Nordskov."

"Good to hear, that's where I keep my money." His dad laughed at his own joke.

"I like to hear that." Tess smiled at his dad.

"Tess comes from New Paris. It's down by Rochester," Dolly told her husband, apparently making her an expert on the subject.

"I've never heard of that town, but Rochester is far away," Mick chimed in.

"It is not very big," Tess said to the group.

"Didn't you say you went to private school? Was it in your little town?" Mia asked.

"It was not in the town I lived in. It was in the next town over. I drove."

"Wow, private school. What did your dad do to pay for that?" his uncle asked, adding more potatoes to his plate.

Tess stiffened at the question. If they hadn't been pressed together, he wouldn't have felt it. He quickly said, "Tess, you don't have to answer that. It's none of our business."

"No, that is okay. Mr. Lawson, I paid for my own schooling. My father farmed but did not make enough to send me to school," Tess replied, sitting up straighter.

"What?" Math looked at her. Her father farmed, really? No wonder she hadn't complained when he had her help on his farm.

Tess turned her gray eyes to him as she whispered, "Sorry, you were having so much fun that day. I did not want to ruin it for you."

"What does your father farm?" Math's dad asked her. It was a topic he loved to talk about.

Her attention turned from him to his dad. "Small grains mostly and some animals over the years. Now he just helps my brothers; he is retired."

"I hope he's enjoying it. I know I am." Math's dad laughed.

"He is. Whether Mama does is a different story." Tess smiled, and the entire table laughed at her joke.

The table broke down in small conversations again, and Math said to her, "So, you lied."

"I never lied. You never asked, just assumed." She couldn't hide her grin as she took a small bite of ham. Just a sliver, mostly.

"That Ms. Fancy Pants has never gotten her boots dirty. Seemed like a reasonable assessment." He cut his ham in half and put one of the pieces on her plate. She scowled at him.

"Ms. Fancy Pants, that is cute." She chuckled, not taking the name as the put-down he had intended it to be.

He was about to say that she was cute, but he stopped himself by taking a bite of bread. Maybe it was because they had sex so recently that it didn't bother him that she had lied. But really, he knew she hadn't *really* lied. The fact that she grew up on a farm made some sense. It's how she had known how to do everything and did it quickly. Ms. Fancy Pants had already done it all before.

Her laugh caught his attention as she talked to Mia. He had missed what was being said on that side of him. On his other side, Mandy was still talking with Kit. He strained his ear, listening to Tess. He caught her whispering, "Shut up," and a laugh but nothing else.

Since he was done eating and he had no room for his arm on the table, he dropped it to his lap. Then as if it had a mind of its own, he slid his hand over her leg. Her legs were crossed under the table, and he put his hand on her knee. There was no reaction from her as he did it, so he left it there. As his uncle drew him into conversation, he kept it there.

Soon she was done eating, and her hand slid over his, not moving it, just holding it. She tensed again when his mom asked her, "Tess, where were you before moving to Landstad?"

She relaxed again and said, "Fargo. I was a personal banker for about ten years."

"Did you like it?" Mandy said from the other side of him.

"I did, but I always wanted more. The last four years there, I was the manager. I was just climbing the ladder." She smiled at Mandy on the other side of him, so he got a glimpse of it as well.

"Do you like it here?" Dotty asked.

"Yes, I do. It is a nice little town. Sometimes I run into people who do not like me, but mostly they are friendly." She squeezed his hand but didn't remove hers from his or look at him.

"Yeah, that's how some people are," Dolly said. She was looking right at Math as she said it.

Tess chuckled at his mom's pointed look. Dropping her hand, he pushed away from the table. "I'm done, so I'm going to go watch the game."

As he entered the living room, he heard others say they were going to join him, but he managed to get to the reclining chair before anyone else came in the room. A fast escape was necessary so that nobody noticed his very pronounced erection, an annoying side effect of being too close to that woman. Or maybe the touching of that woman's warm leg. And the memory of her naked body not two hours before.

Mandy followed him and sat down across from him on the sofa. Turning to her, he said, "Going to take a nap?"

His sister had spent years as a nurse in the ER, then in the NICU before recently coming home to run the clinic in town. Her years of work had left her with the ability to sleep anywhere. Her favorite spot was on the couch during sporting events on the TV.

"Shut up, Math. I wouldn't start a fight. I have dirt on you," she replied, pulling a throw over her body, not even pretending she was going to do anything else.

"What dirt do you have?" His other sister Kit walked into the room, holding her two-year-old. She had separated from her second husband during her last pregnancy, so she was constantly exhausted, especially today.

Grabbing the boy from her, he asked, "Yeah, what dirt?"

"Things you maybe don't want me saying out loud today about a phone call I recently got." Mandy arranged the blanket around herself.

"Doctor-patient confidentiality," Math said, settling the boy on his lap. He was just about asleep.

"Neither of you are my patients," Mandy replied with a laugh.

Kit turned to him in excitement. "Did you get someone pregnant?"

"No, good god, no," he answered a little too loudly. The only person he had slept with since his divorce was in the kitchen.

"What then? Mandy?" Kit demanded.

"I'm not saying. I'll keep it to myself until I need a favor. It's nice to have something over my brother's head.

"Is it about Tess? He was pretty happy to be next to her while we ate. And he actually talked to her," Kit said, her expression thoughtful.

"Not going to say." Mandy yawned.

"Does it have anything to do with the fact I haven't heard her say a contraction?" Kit asked eagerly.

Mandy's eyes widened. "Doesn't she?"

"What are you talking about?" he asked at the same time.

"You know, a shortened form of words usually using an apostrophe." Kit focused on him as she explained, as if he didn't know that. Then Kit turned back to Mandy, "I don't know why I noticed it, but I did. I guess being a teacher, I pick up on little things,"

Math watched her watch Mandy fall asleep, and then she turned to him, pointing at their sister. "Keep an eye on that one."

"I try," he replied as she walked away. Mandy wasn't the sister he was concerned about these days. Kit's marriage had imploded when she was two months pregnant, and now she had five kids to raise with no help. His sister was up for the task, but the new baby was wearing her down.

Since the boy had fallen asleep in his arms, he decided to try and take a nap as well since everyone else was.

When he next opened his eyes, the boy was gone, and so was Mandy from the couch. Getting up, he decided to go looking for Tess. He was her ride, after all.

Walking into the kitchen, he saw a couple of women sitting at the table talking, but none were Tess—or Mandy or Mia for that matter. Math grabbed a piece of cake and asked casually, "Where are the girls?"

His mom looked at him with a grin. "You mean Tess? Your sister and Mia took her to book club."

"No, Mom. All the girls, not just that one."

"You seemed pretty interested in her today," Dotty said from the table.

"I was not. I was trying to be friendly. Isn't that what you guys wanted?" He was no longer hungry for the cake he had taken.

"It's not what we want, Math. It's what you want," his mother replied nonchalantly.

"I bet," he said, leaving the room with his cake.

Math went back to sit in his recliner, but he couldn't pay attention to the game. She had snuck away while he slept. But since she had book club, he couldn't rush over to her apartment to see if she would let him in again. Of course, he had his kids anyway, so that plan was out. Mia and his mom had taken them here when they made Math go get Tess, but he was taking them home.

The woman had been infuriating from the moment she'd opened the door, phone to her ear. The argument about her not joining his family for the holiday had been heated, too heated. By the time he had gotten her back literally against the wall, he couldn't keep his hands or lips to himself. Her response had been as heated as his own. Once he had gotten her into the bedroom, he knew there was no stopping.

Remembering her arguing with him, naked with just-had-sex hair, made him groan out loud. In his lifetime, he had never had an argument with a naked woman, let alone a sexy, naked woman. But that woman could argue no matter where she was or what she was wearing. It was a turn-on.

He was glad he had brought her with him to dinner. She had fit in with the large group as if she came over there every weekend, holding babies and making jokes with his parents and aunt and uncle. For some reason, she just fit in—maybe too well, based on his mother's comments.

He needed to ignore her for a while. Or maybe he should just stop by one night to see how book club went. Or maybe not; the more time he spent with her, the more perfectly she fit into his life. And she wasn't supposed to have a place in his life.

CHAPTER 12

"I say at least seven," Natasha whispered in Tess's ear.

Turning to her oldest friend, Tess held up six fingers, then pointed at a possible one from her spot in the middle of a large group of people in the church, trying not to be obvious about the accusation.

"Not Katya, she just had one," Natasha whispered to her.

"Does not matter," Tess said about her twenty-four-year-old niece sitting in front of them. The women were playing their favorite church game: how many in their family would have a baby by the next time this holiday rolled around. They had been doing it since they found out how babies were made, about the time the family really started to expand. The game never got old. With their massive family, there were always women pregnant.

The atmosphere was a little different from the week before, with Mia in Math's Lutheran church. This was more formal and much longer. It had already been an hour, and the service wasn't even halfway over. Everybody was in attendance today, from her parents to Ilya's newest grandbaby. It was always fun to see everyone, even though it was a little overwhelming as their numbers grew every year.

Last week at this time, she was with Mathias's family. It had been more fun than she had expected it to be. Mandy and Mia were always fun to spend time with, but Mathias had been on his best behavior all day. Well, except at church and then at her apartment when they were fighting … and maybe the after-church sex should not have happened.

All week she thought that she would hear from him, like it had been a date or something. But nothing. By Friday, when she drove out of town, she had slowly given up hope of seeing him. The sex definitely shouldn't have happened.

But today, she was with her family, and he wouldn't bring her down. Next to Tess sat her brother, Sergey, who shushed them. Tess looked at him and rolled her eyes. He cracked a smile at her.

Excusing herself, she headed to the bathroom in the basement, needing a break. An hour-long church service sounded pretty appealing right then. Once she was done in the bathroom, she hung out for a little bit in the basement, away from the steady monotone Russian of the priest. She needed to get away from the stifling heat, thankful for her white sundress.

"Terezilya, what are you doing down here?" Ilya asked as she came down the stairs. Her sister was just an older version of Tess, leaving Tess no doubt what she would look like in eight years. Luckily, she would be aging gracefully.

"Going to the restroom," Tess stated, but she was looking at a picture on the wall across from the restroom, which had its door open, revealing that no one was using it.

"Me too," Ilya replied, but her tone told Tess her sister thought she should be in the pews upstairs.

Then Ilya went into the nearby restroom.

Tess waited for her sister to leave the bathroom to walk up with her, but when her sister came out, she looked Tess up and down. Tess wondered if her sister didn't think her dress was church-appropriate.

"What is wrong, Terezilya?" Her sister could always read her moods.

"Nothing," Tess said but sat down on a bench running along the wall.

Ilya sat next to her. "Talk to me. What is it?"

"I think I am going through menopause," Tess whispered.

"What?" Her sister sounded as shocked as Tess felt about it.

"The change; the end," Tess tried to explain.

"I know what it is, Terezilya. I have already gone through it, but you are not old enough."

"The internet says any time after thirty-five. I am thirty-seven."

"The internet does not know. I just started going through the change a few years ago, and mama had you at forty-two. Thirty-seven is too young in our family," Ilya argued, shaking her head.

"But it has stopped." Tess bit her lip. It had been years since she had talked to her sister about periods, yet it was still just as uncomfortable as when she was in high school.

"Could be another reason. Have you seen a doctor?"

"No, I just started to worry about it. I do not think it is a doctor kind of thing if I am just getting old." Maybe she should stop in and see Mandy at the clinic one day. Mandy would know; she is a nurse practitioner.

"You are not old enough. See a doctor and make sure it is not..." Ilya stopped dead and stared at Tess, eyes wide.

"Cancer?" Tess said the word her sister couldn't.

"Do not talk like that, Terezilya. You are fine." Ilya looked at Tess and asked quietly, "Could you be pregnant?"

"No way," she replied quickly. Of course, it wasn't that. Sure, she had sex recently, but she had been on the pill, and they had used a condom. And it was only last week that they relied only on the pill. There was no way she was pregnant.

Ilya hugged her little sister. "Go to a doctor and have them look. Then call me."

"I will," she said as her sister got up.

"Come up when you are ready." Ilya squeezed her hand and went back to the service.

Tess followed soon after, wondering what she was going to do if she had cancer. Who would take care of her when she got really sick? Would she be able to work? The first thing would be to get into the Mayo Clinic in Rochester; it was only an hour from her family. Then she would have to decide about her job, her friends, and her life.

After sliding into the pew next to Tasha, she noticed that her friend was cradling her youngest and trying to get the little girl to sleep. Tess did her best to hold back tears as she wondered whether Natasha's kids would remember her when she was gone. How would her mom handle burying another child? She had lost four back in Russia, and Tess knew it still bothered her that they were so far away, buried in a cemetery where nobody remembered them. Would that be her?

She had done nothing in her life, and now it was about to be over. Sure, she had some jobs, but they weren't her family, people who loved you no matter what.

Cancer.

Tasha leaned into her with the baby in her arms. Natasha's husband leaned over his wife and handed her a tissue. "Why are you crying? The service is not that good."

"Nothing." She wiped her cheeks and blew her nose quietly.

"Hormones," Tasha stated with a nod but stayed leaned against her as she silently cried through the rest of the Easter Service.

Once the service was over, everyone got up and got out of the sanctuary as fast as possible in case the priest came back out. Tasha stayed, holding her sleeping baby in her arms. Tess stayed because her life would soon be over. She was dying. She needed God more today than any other day.

"Why are you crying?" Tasha asked, still in a whisper, even if there was nobody else there.

"I do not want to talk about it."

"You have never cried in church before, so spill it," her niece demanded quietly. They were still in church, and she was holding a sleeping baby.

"I am dying," Tess whispered and covered her face with a tissue.

"*What?*" Tasha asked, her eyebrow raising in confusion.

"Cancer. I just have to find a doctor to confirm it."

"Self-diagnosed?" Tasha questioned, her brow raising a little higher.

"No, Ilya mentioned it." Because her older sister was a wise older woman, it had to be true.

"I do not think you have cancer, Tessy. Ilya can not know if you have cancer," Tasha said.

"But I do. I thought I was going through menopause, but Ilya said I was too young. It has to be cancer," Tess explained.

"So, cancer. Not the obvious other answer?" Tasha bumped her shoulder with hers.

She wiped her face with the tissue. "I do not know the obvious answer, Tasha."

"Let's see." Tasha turned to her with the baby draped over her. She looked Tess up and down. "Puffy face, bigger boobs—I bet they are sensitive too. And you're overly emotional. I haven't seen you cry since we were kids, and this weekend it has happened twice."

"So, what does that mean?" Tess demanded, slightly annoyed her niece was pointing out her weaknesses. How could she not cry when she saw her mom after so many months? Just because it had never happened before didn't matter.

Tasha touched the cheek she claimed was puffy, saying, "I noticed it yesterday when you woke up. You're knocked up."

"I am *not*," she insisted. "It is cancer, Tasha. I am dying."

Tasha just shook her head, "I can spot a pregnant Aleksandrov at a hundred feet. You have the look."

"You counted *me* as seven?" Tess demanded, not knowing who that last one could have been.

"Oh, yes. I assume it happened on your birthday after a night of drinking with your friends. With that guy who doesn't like you," Tasha stated, bouncing the baby to keep her asleep.

"That was the only time, but we used protection—the pill and a condom. This was not supposed to happen," Tess insisted, bewildered.

Things like unwed pregnancy happened to others, not her. She was the smart one, the one to be dedicated to her job for the family. It was why cancer made sense with her symptoms, even the ones she didn't tell Ilya about. But she had never been pregnant before, not even a scare. How was she supposed to know?

"Nor was this, but it happens. And I am so excited." Tasha pointed to the baby in her arms.

"Mama and Papa will kill me." Tess leaned back in the pew, hiding her face with her hands.

"You are not a kid, Tessy. They will be so excited to see you as a mom. They are not as strict as they used to be. They have mellowed. Mikhail will have a few words to say, but then they will all get over it. A baby helps with that." Tasha maybe knew better. She was around them all the time.

"If I really am pregnant, I cannot tell them yet. I have to figure out things on my end first," Tess said.

"Good luck. The others will figure it out soon. I just see you more often with FaceTime, so I see the changes." Tasha smiled at her and patted her cheek with her one free hand.

"Thanks. Puffy cheeks." She touched one herself.

"They are so round and cute, Tessy. What will the daddy say? Will he get a say?" Tasha shifted the baby in her arms.

"No need to rush into telling him if it's cancer after all, so I need to know for sure before I even think about saying anything. There is for sure no us, and I would assume he will be mad when I tell him about this. I just might not tell him," Tess admitted. Maybe it was for the best. Math had no real long-term interest in her, so why would he be interested in her baby? He already had three kids. Would he even want another one?

"It's your call. You have the means to support a baby without a husband. But maybe you want some support anyway," Tasha said.

The two sat in silence until Alex came and told his wife they had to get home. Since Tess had driven herself, she continued to sit and think that just an hour ago she was dying alone, and now she was maybe carrying someone to love forever in her stomach.

She wondered whether or not to tell Mathias. She assumed he would be mad that it had happened, that she let it happen. He would most likely be mad that he would be saddled with her for a lifetime; he didn't like her on the best of days. But if she kept it from him, he would hate her if he ever found out.

No matter what she did, he most likely would hate her anyway.

CHAPTER 13

THE NEXT MORNING, Tasha had her take a pregnancy test. Positive. Tasha squealed with delight and danced while Tess panicked even more and hid her tears. Now it was more real than before. Maybe it was still cancer.

Weeks before, she had scheduled a job interview in a town during her long drive back to Landstad. It was for a bank president in a town just a few hours from her parent's house. It was still farther away than they would travel to see her but closer for her to visit. She had felt it went pretty well, and it would be best to get out of Landstad. This way, if she never told Math about the baby, he would never have to know. And if she did tell him, and he didn't want it, she wouldn't have to see him afterward.

Now it had been three days since she'd found out she was pregnant, and she couldn't stop thinking about the baby and everything it meant. Trying to take her mind off the big questions, she headed down to the café for a late lunch. It was a rare treat when she let herself eat at a restaurant. Probably too many years of her parents declaring it was a waste of money. Most of the time, she brought a lunch to work, and today was no different. But with the sun shining and Tess needing some fresh air, she headed to the café.

The air was crisper than it had looked through the bank windows, and Tess wished she had worn her coat, but she was nearly at the door of the café. She finally pushed through the door, happy to feel the warmth surround her.

"Tess Thorn, are you darkening my door during a workday?" Mia asked from a booth by the door with a grin, reminding Tess that she rarely went out to eat in town.

"I can leave if you do not want me here," Tess said, wishing she had just stayed in her office.

"No, no. Come and have a seat. I was just keeping Hazel company, but now you can." Mia jumped up from the table and indicated that Tess should take her place.

Tess glanced at Hazel, relieved that maybe she wouldn't have to sit alone until she realized she had never had a one-on-one with the younger woman. They had always been together in the larger group.

As Tess slid into the booth, she smiled at Hazel. "No John Henry today?"

Hazel's four-year-old son was almost always with her unless it was book club night, which meant that Tess had seen very little of him up close. All she knew was that he looked a lot like his thin, blonde mother.

"No, there's a thing at the school for his age group today, so I'm waiting for it to get done." She lived in the country and probably didn't want to make the trip into town again.

Tess always liked quiet Hazel; she was one of those shy people until you got a few drinks in her or she got comfortable with you. Then she was a fireball.

"Does he like it?" Tess toyed with the menu as she spoke, not opening it.

"I don't know; it's his first one," Hazel admitted.

Mia came back to them and asked Tess what she wanted. Only then did Tess look at the menu. After she ordered a bowl of soup, Mia made a comment about how cheap Tess was before walking away.

"What is it like being a single mom?" Tess ignored the waitress and turned back to Hazel. She was her only friend in that category, and suddenly, she wanted to know more about it. It was all she had thought about for days now.

"It's okay." Hazel's expression said she was curious as to why Tess was asking.

"Have you always been?"

"Yes. The father was never a part of it."

Tess nodded slowly. "Did you want him to be?"

"He didn't really get a choice on it since I didn't know who he was," Hazel admitted, taking Tess by surprise. There was a side of Hazel she had never expected.

Mia brought her soup and sat down with Hazel. "How was your trip?"

"Good, I got to see everyone." Tess did not elaborate on who everyone was.

"Well, you missed nothing around here. The town was dead all weekend," Mia said as she saw someone come in, and she jumped up to talk to them. Mia had more energy than anyone Tess had ever seen.

Hazel watched the waitress walk away, but then her eyes flicked back to Tess. "Why all the questions, Tess?"

"I am pregnant, and I have to decide if I am going to tell the father," Tess hesitantly replied as she looked around to see if anyone was sitting close by. She didn't want the entire town to know just yet, or maybe ever.

"Wow," Hazel said, her eyes wide.

"Hazel, you have been where I am at. Do you have any advice?"

Hazel took a drink from her water glass. "I have never been where you're at. I was nineteen and in my second year of college, and I couldn't find the dad if I tried. You are successful and can support a baby without the dad or anyone else."

"So, no advice then?"

"My advice is that if you want the father at the baby's graduation or wedding one day, you have to tell him. If it doesn't matter, then don't. If you want him to change diapers, that is completely different. And if he says he wants nothing to do with the baby or you, then screw him—that baby is yours. I love my baby, with or without his dad. I wouldn't trade him for anything," Hazel said as she watched Mia walk around the café.

"You are right, Hazel." Tess looked out the window at the semi-busy street.

"Do you like the father?" Hazel asked.

Tess looked back at her and grinned. "Sometimes. We fight all the time."

All? Hazel tried to hide a smile behind her water glass.

"No, not all. But we are definitely not in the 'we want to have a kid together' place in our relationship." Tess sighed.

"Have you tried dating?"

"No."

"Then go on a date and see if he is someone you want in your life forever. Might be all it takes to figure it out," Hazel said as Mia came back to sit by them.

"See? You had advice for me after all," Tess said. She set her glass down on the wooden table and looked up again. "Can we keep this between us, Hazel? At least for a while?"

"What if you decide not to tell him, but he realizes the baby is his?" Hazel asked.

Tess shook her head. "He will never know. I have applied for a job closer to my family. I cannot have the baby here alone."

"You're leaving?" Hazel put down her glass in surprise.

"Possibly."

Mia walked up to the table and sat down, this time by Tess. Once again, the waitress dominated the conversation. She didn't notice that neither of the women were actually involved in the conversation she was having. Tess glanced at her watch and realized she needed to get back to the bank. Interrupting her friend, explaining that she had to leave, and Mia only barely let her out of the booth.

"Are you going to become a regular?" Mia asked as she followed her to the cash register.

"I do not know." Tess paid her bill, knowing she wasn't coming back unless she needed to talk again. Though she didn't think she would have gotten the advice she had from anyone but Hazel.

Handing back her change, Mia replied, "You're always welcome, and thanks for sitting with Hazel. She was a little nervous about sending John Henry to the school thing. I wish I had time to talk to you, but a waitress called in sick, so I'm stuck alone."

"That is fine. Hazel and I had a good talk. She helped me with more than anyone I thought possibly could," Tess acknowledged as she headed out the door and back to work.

CHAPTER 14

THE MIDDAY SUN was warm and bright, beating down on Math as he glared at the puddles in the yard from the overnight rain. Today was shot for farming; the fields were too wet to do anything. He could only watch the puddles dry and hope it didn't rain again.

It had been just over a week since he had slid that white dress over Tess's head with her sex-mussed hair. Over a week since he had touched her, kissed her, and he wanted to do it again. Over a week was turning into too long to touch her again. He didn't think he could go months this time.

He knew she was back in town yesterday because her car was parked on the street when he had dropped the kids off at school that morning. He had shaken his head at the bank president's little old Chevrolet. It didn't fit her position in town, but it really seemed to fit her personality perfectly.

So far, he hadn't seen her, not that he went out of his way to see her. He knew she was at the bank, but he hadn't found an excuse to go in there to see if her trip went okay. He didn't want it to look like he was just going into the bank to see her.

Who would have thought there were two Easters? He had read up on her religion, and he almost asked the pastor about it on Sunday after services since he'd seemed to know about it when talking to Tess the weekend before. But he kept his mouth shut; he wasn't that interested.

Kicking a rock, he tried to get her out of his mind. Really it had been less than two weeks, but his mind wouldn't let go of the memory of her naked body. Naked and arguing with him, then making love to him. He couldn't get her out of his mind.

His cell phone rang in his pocket, causing him to stop. Pulling it out he didn't recognize the phone number on the display; it wasn't local. He answered it anyway, maybe something about the kids. "Math Nordskov."

"Mathias, it is Tess Thorn at Landstad Bank," the woman said as if she had to say anything beyond her name for him to know who it was.

"Hello, Tess." He couldn't stop a smile from spreading across his lips.

"I got your number from Mandy. I hope you don't mind."

"That was fine."

"I was wondering if you would be interested in having supper with me one evening this week." Her slow cadence was even slower than it usually was. Was she nervous?

"Are you asking me out on a date, Thorn?" he asked with a smile. He could see her gray eyes closing.

"No!" she said quickly, and his phone went dead. She had hung up on him.

Looking at his phone, he laughed at the idea she had been so nervous that she hung up. So, he called the number back. He was surprised when she actually answered, though she was as formal as before. "Tess, it's Math Nordskov from my farm."

"Hello, Mathias. What can I do for you?" she said as if they hadn't just been on the phone, and she hadn't just asked him out and hung up on him.

"Hello, Tess. I got your number from when you just called me." He mirrored her earlier call, and he loved that it made her chuckle.

"I guess I deserve that." She sighed into her phone, into his ear, and the sound went straight to his dick.

"Yes, I would like to go out with you."

"When?"

"Are you at work?"

"Yes," she answered hesitantly.

"Can you get away early?" He had nothing else to do.

"I can, but give me an hour. Do you want me to pick you up?" she asked. He could tell she was moving papers around on her desk.

"No, I will not ride in that rust bucket you drive." His mind went to the red car. "I expected the bank's president to drive something a bit fancier."

"She *is* fancy. She has a CD and a tape player." She chuckled into the phone, and he loved the sound.

"She's a stick shift." He remembered from the day she had worked on his farm.

"I know, she is a sports car." There was a smile in her voice.

"Teenagers drive better cars."

"Only the lucky ones. It is a great car. I bought it new," she said as she continued to move papers.

"I bet you could get a loan for another one. You seem to have connections," he said and laughed.

"I bet I have another five years in this one. And I do not do loans." He could tell her attention had moved away from him because she wasn't concentrating on what she was saying anymore.

"So, you have never had a loan?" he questioned since that was her business.

"Sorry, I was reading something. What did you say?"

He could tell her attention was back. He repeated his question, and she said in response, "No, I see too many people who rely on them. I never want to do that to myself. But I have to go. See you in an hour."

She hung up on him without saying goodbye. How did she get to be her age and never have a loan? She had to be lying. But to what point?

Math hurried into the house since he only had an hour to get ready. Finally, he had his reason to spend time with her, all without him even stepping foot in the bank again. He had been sure that if he had walked in there, she would have shot him down in front of the entire town. So, her calling had been perfect, beyond perfect.

On top of that, his kids were with his ex tonight, so he didn't have to worry about finding somewhere for them to go. There was nothing standing between him and this woman, and he was definitely going on this date. Math didn't know if she had a date planned or if he was supposed to be planning that. Maybe she would just take him up to her apartment and have her way with him? That was exactly what he wanted, to see that tattoo again.

Less than an hour later, he had showered, shaved, and changed, all in record time before driving into town. As he hit the city limits, he wondered if he should pick her up at the bank or at her apartment. She hadn't said. Thankfully, they were a block apart, so he would be able to find her in a short amount of time.

His worrying was for nothing because she was leaning against the wall in front of the drug store below her apartment, waiting. He was sure she had changed because she was now wearing form-fitting black jeans and a white blouse, an outfit far more casual than the ones he knew she wore to work. She had a jacket draped over her arm for later.

Before she could open the door, he slid the window down and said, "What's the plan, Thorn?"

Her smile faltered as she leaned into the window. "I had not thought of that. What do people usually do?"

Leaning over, he opened the door latch for her, loving that her smell was already permeating his truck. "We have time to go to Grand Forks for something to eat."

She looked over at him with a frown as she climbed in. "That is over an hour away."

"Yes, it is." He wanted to touch her as she closed the door and put on her seatbelt, but he held himself back. No need to scare her right away.

"I just mean it is a long way to just eat." She finally looked up and smiled.

"We're not in the big city, so there's little else out here." He put the truck in gear and headed out of town.

As town disappeared behind them, he realized this was the first date he had been on since his divorce. Well, the first one he had wanted to be on. Before, when he had thought about dating, it just seemed overwhelming and uncomfortable. But Tess beside him felt natural, right. Perfect.

"I am not from the big city," she argued as she looked out the window at the still black fields. "New Paris is bigger than Landstad but far from a big city."

Reaching over, he tucked a lock of her hair behind her ear. "So, your parents were poor farmers. How did you pay for private school?"

Whether it was the touch or the question, her demeanor changed instantly, and she turned to look out the passenger window. Math put his hand back on the steering wheel, regretting bringing it up. He hated that she was suddenly not happy, wanting her smile back.

CHAPTER 15

HIS QUESTION MADE HER CRINGE, even if she knew he would bring it up. She had just hoped they would make it further from town before he asked. Nothing she had said that day was a lie, but she had purposefully not told him about her past. After their first few encounters, she felt it was wise not to get too personal with him since she was sure he would use anything she told him against her.

But that was until she realized how connected they now were and would be until the end of time, which meant she had to prove to him that they weren't as different as he wanted to believe. That they had more than one little thing in common.

So instead of glossing over the entire situation with her childhood, she told him the truth. "I saved my money, took extra jobs, and worked my tail off every summer. And I got a few scholarships. My parents did not have any extra money in those days, nor did they want me to go. I took it upon myself, and I secretly enrolled and told them later," she said with a smile. It wasn't something she was overly proud of, but it had gotten her what she'd wanted.

"You did not." He chuckled and seemed to relax more into the conversation, his one hand finally leaving the steering wheel.

When she had called, she was sure he would say no. In fact, she was sure he would say hell no, which meant she hadn't been even close to ready to go out today, right away. She had assumed it would be a weekend thing.

"What would you do if Cora enrolled herself in school?" She kicked off her heels and slid one foot under her leg. It was a long drive.

"I would be shocked because she barely wants to go to the school she is in. But I don't think she would have the know-how to enroll herself into anything," Math admitted about his oldest daughter, then smiled at her. "I love her, but I also know her."

"Do not underestimate a teenager with a dream. I was her age." She loved his smile and loved it even more when it was aimed at her.

"She's fifteen," he reminded her.

"Yes, I know. I was fifteen. I wanted to go to private school for my junior and senior years." She was paying more attention to him driving than to the scenery going by them. He was looking very good this afternoon in jeans and a gray button-up shirt, two buttons undone.

"What did your parents say? Why didn't you just ask them?"

"I did ask, but my father said the public school was good enough. It took a while for them to find out. My sister helped me enroll since she was eight years older than me and had three kids with her. Which meant they never questioned if I was hers or not. A month later, when Mama and Papa found out I was already in classes, it was paid for, and to unenroll me would have been a hassle for them. I was punished and went on with my life. They never said anything about it again, not even the next year. Or later." She looked out at the freshly planted black fields.

They still didn't talk about it, ever. The only indication that she graduated from anything was a picture on the wall of her in her graduation gown. But they did not take the picture, Tasha did. They did not attend the ceremony, nor was there a party afterward. She didn't even know if they knew she graduated third in her class … probably not.

"They never said anything?" he asked in surprise and reached over to squeeze her knee for a second before pulling away just as fast.

"Oh, sometimes someone will mention the fancy school I went to, but they could also be talking about college. I was the first in my family to attend a fancy college also. I do not know and do not care anymore." She then changed the subject, tired of talking about her family or about how much different her family was from other families. "So, are you done planting yet?"

"Not yet. A few more days, but it was too wet today. See? I was not busy, Tess Thorn from the bank." He reached over and squeezed her knee again but left his hand there this time. His hand was warm, and it sent tingles throughout her body.

"It is just how I introduce myself on the phone. And I did not know if you would recognize my voice."

"Because of any other Tesses that might call?" He grinned at her.

"Sorry." He probably hadn't wanted her to call either; he was just being polite.

"I knew it was you when you called me Mathias. Nobody but you calls me that," he informed her.

"Really? Nobody? But it is your name, and it is so nice," she asked in confusion.

"Thank you, but I have always just been Math. Has it always been Tess?"

"What? How did you know?" She stared at him.

"I didn't, but when you were passed out, someone texted you and called you Tere.… I don't know how you pronounce it," he said.

"It is just short form of Teresa. My sister says it takes too long to type my whole name out," she admitted.

"But she doesn't call you Tess, which is also short for Teresa?"

"No, she never has." Of course, nor did she call her Teresa, ever.

"So, Teresa Alexandra Sophia Thorn?"

Tess was surprised he had remembered her middle names. She bit her lip because she wanted to correct it for him, to have him say her name as her parents had named her and not the Americanized version. But instead, she said, "Yes."

They pulled up to a chain restaurant, and Tess was surprised the ride had seemed so short. They had actually gotten along very well. Better than she had expected. But she was waiting for the bomb to drop to where he couldn't stand her again. It always seemed to happen.

As they were led to a table, Math's hand rested on her back, shifting around slightly as she moved. It was just enough to send a shiver down her spine. God, her body craved his touch.

Menus were handed out, and they were looking over them when Math asked, "Do you see anything that looks good, Teresa?"

She set her menu down, slapping his to the table as well. "Do not call me that. It is not my name anymore."

"You can't just quit your name," he argued.

"I can, and I did. I have my reasons," she stated and drank from the water glass in front of her.

"Then give me one. Then I will decide if I'll drop it. Maybe I'll keep calling you that until you stop calling me Mathias." He was grinning as he said it.

"I have a sister-in-law who shares my name, and I cannot stand her. And I do believe you like that I call you Mathias." It was also her mother's name, as well as four of her nieces and countless great-nieces. It was a common name in her family. That was truly why she didn't use it anymore.

He stared at her for a minute, just staring at her with his blue eyes. They were making her feel uncomfortable. "I will not call you anything but Tess. I do like you calling me Mathias. It sounds different when you say it."

Just then, the waitress came back to take their orders. She told the woman what she wanted and then watched Mathias place his order. Had he just told her to call him by his name because she said it was nice? What did that mean? She only called him that because she, like her sister, called people by their given names. It was only after a while that she used nicknames, if ever. Mandy had been introduced as just Mandy, so she doesn't think of her as Amanda.

"Can I ask you some questions?" he asked when the waitress was gone.

"Sure, as long as I can ask some too."

"Why do you live uptown? Why not a house? You have been in town for over a year. Shouldn't you be thinking about settling in?" He leaned forward and rested his elbows on the table.

"Uptown, I like that. Sounds classy." She smiled at him. "I moved in there because it was convenient and close to the bank. I was going to look for bigger later, but after a while, I liked walking to work and having everything right there. Why move and have to start my car on bitterly cold days and have to mow a lawn?"

"But isn't it small?"

"Yes, but cozy, I guess. I have never had a large place. Small and cheap is what I like."

"Except your clothes." His eyes dropped to her shirt, or maybe her breasts. She couldn't tell.

"You noticed? Yes, I like to dress nice. It is my money to spend," she defended her spending habits. "Now me. Where did you come up with Juniper's name?"

Math smiled. "Mandy came up with it. She's really good at naming babies. Karen and I had no idea what to name her, and Mandy just started calling her that. It was her perfect name."

"I like your sister," Tess said, happy that Mandy was in book club with her. From the first day, she reminded Tess of Natasha—fun and caring.

"Me too. I have two others kind of like her," he said.

"I met Kit at Easter; is it short for Katrina? Do you all look the same? You and Mandy and Kit have similar coloring."

"Kit is short for Kristiana. Yes, we all look the same. Julia is tall like Kit."

"Your kids look like you as well." She wondered if the baby she was carrying would be a constant reminder of him. "Have you always wanted to farm?"

"Oh, yeah, since I was younger than Mason, but I know he has no interest in it. I didn't even go to college; I just started to work for my father. I love it."

"It sounds like it. I like when people are happy with their work."

"Do you miss your family, living so far away? Julia lives in Fargo, which is too far for a regular visit." His expressive blue eyes were on her.

"Yes, I miss them. I do talk to someone from there every day. Most days I talk to Tasha, but I talk to my mother and sister also. My brother calls too often. I have gotten used to it over the years," she replied, though she didn't keep track of who she talked to during the day. She was sure it was more than two most days.

"Who is Tasha? And did you talk to her today?"

"Tasha is my niece. Yes, I sent her a text right before you picked me up, so you cannot kill me since she knows I am with you." Tess laughed at his pained expression.

"Does she know who I am?"

"Yes, we have no secrets."

"Wait, is she the one you kept texting when you were on drugs?"

"Yes, and it was not the first time she has gotten medication texting from me." She laughed. She had read her texts after those two days; she had quite the trip.

"But not drunk texts? Because you don't get drunk." He laughed at her.

"I know you do not believe me. She is the drunk texter. She cannot handle her booze, but she has Alex, so she does not have to." She sighed at her friend's relationship. She wanted the kind of relationship Tasha had.

"But not you?"

"I have not been drunk since I was seventeen, and I do not plan to do it again. That was a day." She laughed at herself—Tasha's wedding was just a blur.

"What happened that day?"

"Tasha and Alex got married. Then we celebrated, and my brother and I had a drinking contest, of which I won. And then my dad challenged me, and he won." She drank her water.

"Did they not remember you were seventeen?"

"It was a wedding. You drink at weddings."

"Always?" He looked into her eyes, shocked.

"Always." She looked back into his blue eyes, smiling.

"How old were you when you first drank at a wedding?"

"Ten. Ilya got married, and Tasha and I got wasted. But she is a lightweight, hence the drunk texts." She laughed.

"Prove it," he challenged.

Just then, the food arrived, breaking their eye contact. Looking at her meal, she wondered if she had actually ordered what was in front of her. Math had already started eating and was watching her. She hated eating in front of people. Over the years, she had actually been able to avoid it almost completely, but here she was, and Mathias was already watching her. Judging her.

As she picked up the knife and fork, she realized she had already eaten in front of him three times. What was one more? He hadn't made fun of her the last time, just gave her more food. She just smiled back and took a bite of chicken, hoping he would stop watching her.

It did not work. He was just going to watch her eat. "Stop watching me."

"I can't. You ordered a chicken burger, and you're cutting it up. Just like the hotdog."

She set her silverware down. "Please do not make fun of the way I eat."

"I'm not making fun of you, Tess. I am stating a fact. If you don't want to draw attention to yourself, don't order the burger. Maybe just order the chicken?" He shrugged and took another bite from his dinner.

"Because if you do not order the burger, you do not get lettuce and tomato. I happen to like that part." Folding her arms, she knew he wouldn't understand.

"Okay, how about this? Next time you order what you want, and I will give you my lettuce and tomato from my burger. Then you can have it the way you like," he said.

"I like the bread too." She couldn't believe he had not only said next time but also that he would give her something she liked just because she wanted it.

"And you like the chicken." He smiled at her.

"No, I do not really like chicken, but it's healthy. I try to eat healthy," she admitted and laughed with him.

"You want my burger, don't you?" he asked in feigned fear, holding it close to his body.

"No, Mathias, you can keep your burger. It is very unhealthy." But it was what she should have ordered, what she wanted to order.

"The unhealthiness is what makes it good," he answered as she picked up her silverware again.

"If you can take a bite without cutting it up, I will let you try it."

Looking up at him, she saw he was holding the juicy-looking burger toward her. Reluctantly, she took it from him and took a big bite, bigger than she should have, which was why she used the fork and knife. Handing it back, she noticed him watching her again, waiting for her reaction.

Wiping her face with the napkin, she laughed. "Thank you, Mathias. It is good."

He smiled happily. "And I got to see you eat with your hands."

To her surprise, he took his burger and put it on her plate and took her chicken sandwich and put it on his. Then he removed the lettuce and tomato and put them on her plate also.

"Mathias, no. You eat your burger; you ordered it." She looked at the burger and the extra vegetables on her plate. The burger made everything look more appetizing.

"I don't remember what I ordered. Must be what is on my plate. And you can eat it any way you want to," he said, taking a bite of the dry chicken sandwich and winking at her.

"Now I owe you something." She picked up her knife and fork again.

"You do. I'm waiting for proof that you drank at ten," he reminded her.

"How? There are no pictures." She took a bite of the burger, smaller this time because she was using her fork.

"Text your friend. She can either confirm or deny it." He pointed to her phone.

"Tasha?"

"Her. Ask her when she said you first drank. No asking if your story was true; she needs to give the number," he said and watched her eat a French fry with her fork.

"Okay." She set down the silverware again and texted her niece the question. When a text came in, she laughed. "She says she will not answer until she gets a picture of you, proof you exist."

"Okay, as long as I get an answer," he replied and smiled as she took his picture. She sent it to Tasha and waited.

"Now we wait. She gets busy sometimes," she said of her friend, then added, "Thank you for coming out with me. I did not think you would."

Mathias took a bite of fry and chewed slowly before replying, "I really should have asked you. I owe you an apology for Easter. I was just surprised to see you. You said you were going home, and I didn't apologize that day."

"I guess I did not think about it. I am used to it being a different day, and I forget most people do not realize it is. I have never been invited to someone else's Easter before," Tess tried to explain. Maybe she should have taken more time talking to him and not having sex with him.

Then a text came in, after she glanced at it she chuckled.

"What did she say?" He tried to look at her phone from across the table.

"She says that Alex, her husband, says you are too blond to be trusted." She turned the phone so that he could read it himself.

"Me? You're blonde too. Maybe darker, but still blonde. What does this Alex look like?" Math demanded.

"He looks like me." She laughed as another text came in.

"Like you?"

"Yes, he is my nephew," she said, reading the text.

"I thought that Tasha was your niece?" He looked at her phone with an eyebrow raised in question.

Tess closed her eyes and stopped laughing. She had stumbled. Leaning back in her seat, she set down her phone. There was no way he would understand that her niece and nephew were married, even if she was a step-niece. Other families didn't have things like that happen, just hers.

"Well, they are married. Like aunt and uncle, only one is truly related to you," she explained, hoping it was a good enough explanation.

"Then which is the one related to you?"

"Alex is my brother's son." It was true, but she always felt closer to Natasha since they were the same age.

"But you have known her your entire life also?"

"Almost, yes." They had met the first day Tess had been in the country.

"It's just different. In my family, all my nieces and nephews are all around the same age. How old is your oldest niece or nephew?" he asked.

Tess tried to think of a way out of that one. She hated when someone pointed out how she was different, odd, weird. But her family made her that way. She opened her eyes again, and she looked at him, right at him to watch his expression. "Forty-three."

"How old are you?" he asked.

"How old are you?" she countered, scoffing.

"Thirty-four, thirty-five around Christmas," he said instantly. She knew he knew when her birthday was.

"I am thirty-seven." She knew he was younger than she was but hadn't known by how much.

"I guess it makes sense that your nieces and nephews are a lot older; you're one sister is eight years older than you. So, the rest must be older than that."

"Yes," she replied. He was being understanding about it. Most people over the years had a lot of questions. Nobody just accepted the truth for what it was.

CHAPTER 16

"Did you get the text back?" He pointed to her phone with a fry. Math had been surprised how her expression had changed when she talked to her family. She was guarded but also just excited. Her childhood seemed very happy from the little she had actually said about it.

She and her niece were so close; he was surprised they rarely saw each other. But they seemed to have an ongoing conversation. He had no idea how to maintain a relationship like that.

Picking up her phone again, she read the text out loud to him, "First time I drink was probably close to eight when we met at that big party. Alex said yes, he drank then too. First time drunk was, of course, Ilya's wedding." She showed him the phone after she had read it.

He took the phone and slipped the fry he was holding into her mouth as he did it. After reading the text, he looked at her over the phone. She was just chewing the fry, looking at him.

It had been the look on her face that made him take her sandwich from her and let her eat his. He wanted her to look at him with the same look she had given that burger—like she had been waiting her entire life to eat that sandwich.

Dragging his eyes from her face and back to the phone, he saw the text was from Nat, just like on her birthday night. Nat had called Tess sweetie. "Why do you have her listed as Nat in your phone?"

"Her name is Natasha," she answered in confusion.

He handed back her phone. "Who is Mike?"

Putting the phone on the table, she looked at him. "Mike, who?"

"You were talking to him the night at the bar on your birthday. He was trying to control you." He wanted to know who thought they could control her, if she *was* controllable. Because he didn't think she was.

"Oh, Mike." She nodded in amusement. "Mike is my brother, the oldest in the family. He tries to control everyone. How do you remember I was talking to Mike?"

"Because it seemed odd that anyone would try and control you or that you would let them," Math said, dropping his napkin on his empty plate.

"I do not let him. Now you see why Mike and I do not get along well." She pushed her plate away from her. It was still half full.

"Is he the drinking contest brother?" He wanted to know if that was the reason for the contest in the first place. He could see a young Tess challenging an older, controlling brother.

"Yes, I have been pushing back against him for a long time now. One day I will win." She laughed a little.

"Why do you think you will win one day?" He wondered what she could do that she hadn't already done? She was a bank president.

"Because he will die first," she stated as the waitress brought the check. She moved to grab it, but he was faster and took it from the waitress. She said as she eyed the check, "I will pay. I invited you out, and you drove."

"Only because I wanted to get here, and I don't trust that car of yours. I will pay because I lost the bet."

Her gray eyes questioned him. "What bet?"

"You were drunk at ten," he replied, slipping his credit card into the envelope and handing it back to the waitress.

"When did you get drunk for the first time?" she asked.

"Probably fifteen or sixteen. I can't remember. It wasn't a big event like a wedding." He really had no idea. He could tell her the place and the time of year, but not how old he was.

"So old," she said as the waitress returned, and they got up to leave the restaurant.

"Just a late bloomer," he replied with a shrug. Then he picked up her leather jacket and slid it onto her soft shoulders before they left the restaurant. It was the same jacket she had worn to the bar on her birthday.

Opening her door for her, he watched as she climbed into his pickup with her heels on. He hoped she would take them off during the drive home. She was a good-looking woman at all times but was even better looking when she was relaxed.

Once he was in the driver's seat and heading out of town again, she kicked her shoes off. All the way home, he let her control the conversation. He knew he had pushed her beyond what she wanted when he was asking about her family. For some reason, she didn't like to talk about them too much. She let them be involved just enough in her life so that they were there, but nothing went too deep. It didn't sound like they ever came to visit her.

"How long were you married?" she asked.

"Thirteen years. She left three years ago."

"So, you were not married long before you had Hailey?" She was leaning her head against the back of the headrest, looking at him.

"Nope, we got married because of Hailey."

"Oh," she said, but he saw she had tensed up.

"Yup. So much for college and all that."

"Sorry. Did you want to go?" she asked, relaxing a little.

"I think I wanted to go to say I went. I don't know if I wanted to go to learn anything," he admitted. Looking back, he knew he would have been a bad student. He was a hands-on kind of guy.

"Did your ex like the farm? Does she miss it?"

"I doubt it; she hated it. She grew up in town."

"Landstad?"

"Yes, we went to school together."

"High school sweethearts?"

He nodded. "We got married before we wanted to, but we got Hailey."

"Cora is a pretty name. Is it a nickname?" she asked.

"No, just her name."

"Math is an odd nickname. And so is Kit."

"Do you have any odd nicknames in your family?" he asked. She was relaxed, but she would talk about her family.

"Not to me, but everyone has the same names. Sometimes a nickname is different, but after a few Alexes, you get used to having one as Al and one as Lex." She was concentrating on her hand. That's when she typically didn't censor her words.

"Your nephew, Alex? Is he Alex?" he asked.

"Yes, only Alex. My brother is Alexei, and papa is just Alex also. But you do not notice they have the same name because nobody calls my father Alex, not even my mother. Always Papa. Grandpa."

"How about Teresa? Are there more Teresas in your family than you and your hated aunt?" he asked, just trying to keep the conversation going, to keep her talking.

"I was named for my mother, so it is everywhere in next generation. My sister has a daughter named Teresa, but we call her Terri. Natasha has one all well, who we call Tessa. She was named after me. And countless others."

"Your best friend named her daughter after you?" He asked, hoping he didn't look as shocked as he felt trying to keep up with the number of Teresas in the family.

"Yes, her second. But it is also after my mother since we share a name." She seemed not to realize she had just said twice that she was named after her mom, but Math wasn't going to point that out.

"Are you named after someone, Mathias?"

"No, Mom just found it in a book, liked it, and here I am," he said. After a moment, he looked over and saw that she had fallen asleep on him.

She was still holding his hand, but she was holding it with both hands. While sleeping, she looked relaxed, better than when she was on the medication for the hives.

In her sleep, she mumbled things that he couldn't understand, just like before. He wondered if she always talked in her sleep, and he hoped he would find out.

CHAPTER 17

IT WAS A DREAM, and Tess knew it. Her daughter was calling her name, her English name. But Tess needed her baby to know that that is not her name, that she had once been Terezilya. She was begging the baby to speak Russian, but the baby just wouldn't do it. *Please just speak Russian, baby. Mama cannot talk to you if you cannot speak Russian.*

"Tess, wake up," she heard right next to her ear.

Opening her eyes, Tess blinked at the man who the baby in her dreams looked like. Looking at Mathias, she wondered if the nightmare would really be her life if she stayed. Would she be able to teach her baby Russian by herself? Would she want to?

"Are you okay?" Mathias asked. He was looking at her in concern.

Shaking her head, she remembered that the baby wasn't even born yet, so she hadn't failed in teaching her anything. But the dream had been too vivid, too real.

Taking a deep breath, she looked around her. They were parked outside her apartment. The street was mostly empty except for the few cars of people who lived downtown. "I am fine. I must have fallen asleep."

"You did. I thought you would rather walk upstairs than have me carry you." His hand was still in hers, so she dropped it.

"Sorry, I must have been sleeping heavy. I usually do not sleep in cars," she explained. Rubbing her hands over her face, she sat up straight. The dream wouldn't diminish.

"Tess, thank you for inviting me out. It was fun," he said. His blue eyes were focused on her, but he wasn't smiling like he had been earlier.

She sighed. "It was, and thank you for paying. Have a nice evening."

"You too."

Turning, she opened the door and got out, hearing him pull away from the curb as she opened the door to her apartment building. She silently cursed herself for falling asleep on him—what a great date she was. *Really smooth, Thorn.* After slamming her door shut, she kicked her shoes off and went to her bedroom to change into yoga pants and a T-shirt since it was only 9:00 pm.

Tess took some files from her briefcase to the couch and sat down, opened one, and tried to look at it. Instead, she closed her eyes and leaned her head against the couch. Today had been her one chance with Mathias, one chance to make him see that she was worth his time, worth getting to know. But instead, she had just managed to make him indifferent toward her. Simply *fun*.

For hours, she had thought it was going well, really well. He had been so nice, like Mandy had said he could be when she had asked her for his number earlier that day. But in the end, he must have realized it was her again. Just Tess, the woman at the bank. The one who denied his loan.

Beside her, the phone rang. With nothing else to do, she answered it without looking at who it was. Without even saying hello to her sister, Ilya was already in the middle of a conversation. There was no preamble with her sister.

"Yes," Tess agreed patiently, not bothering to remind her sister that she had no idea what Ilya was talking about. Tess lived far away from what was happening so close to Ilya, and it made her realize how much she missed being so far away.

Focus, she told herself and sat up to look at the papers again. Tess read the loan application in English and listened to her sister talking in Russian, and she was suddenly proud of herself for making it work. Maybe she wasn't giving either task one hundred percent, but at least eighty on both was good enough for tonight.

Tess had just made a note on the paper when there was a knock on the door, causing her to jump. Closing the file folder, she got up from the couch. "I have to go," she said, but Ilya still continued to talk.

Opening the door, she saw Mathias standing in her hallway. *What was he doing here? He should be halfway home already.* She waved him in, watching him untie his boots and leave them by the door. Meanwhile, her sister continued to talk.

"I have to go," she said again, a little louder this time. He turned to look at her, and she pointed to the phone. "Ilya, I have to go." Ilya still continued to talk.

Rolling her eyes, she saw that he was watching her. God, he was good-looking. Tess pulled the phone away from her ear and hung up on her sister, not for the first time. "Sorry, family."

"I understand. Mine can drive me crazy also." Mathias looked around her apartment as if he had never been there before.

"Sorry, it is a mess." She went over to the coffee table and picked up the folders, putting them in a neat stack before sliding them into her briefcase.

"It's not messy. There's nothing out of place," he replied.

Her phone rang. Glancing at it, she saw it was Ilya. Putting up one finger to Mathias, she answered it, "I told you I was hanging up." Then she hung up again.

"Sorry," she said again, "I thought that you would be almost home by now."

"I'm a bit rusty at this, but I didn't want this to end. Can we talk some more?"

"Do you want to sit?" she asked, trying to control her smile at his words. "A drink?"

"I'll sit, but I don't need anything. You sit," he said as he sat on her couch, making it look small.

Sitting next to him, she breathed in his fresh scent, like the outdoors. "Okay. What do you want to talk about?"

"How long have you been allergic to wheat?" he asked, putting his hand on her thigh. It felt nice.

"Wheat dust. I do not know how long. Maybe always." She shrugged. She had no idea when it started; it was always a thing.

"Anything else you're allergic to? So I don't force you into it." His fingers were making lazy circles on her leg.

"Ragweed when I was younger, but not anymore," she said, smiling. "Are you allergic to anything?"

He laughed. "No, perfectly perfect."

"If you say so, Mathias," she said, looking him up and down. He *was* perfectly perfect.

Taking her hands in his, he looked at them, "They healed okay? You didn't wear gloves that day."

Tess looked at her hands. They looked the same as always. Looking up at him, she said, "Mathias, that was weeks ago. I was fine. A little work has never killed me. I am alive."

"Listen, I'm sorry I made you do all that stuff. I was still a little mad about the loan. I took it out on you," he admitted as he kissed her hands where they had once been red and sore.

"I had fun at your place that day. I have not done so much of that stuff in years. It brought back many memories of my childhood." She smiled at the memory. His attitude hadn't gotten in the way of her having fun that day.

"I can't believe you lied to me about growing up on a farm." He stopped and looked at her, lowering her hands back to her lap.

"I have never lied to you. You, Mathias, never asked."

"Tess, how many times have you shoveled manure?" His hand slid high up on her thigh.

Smiling, she said, "A million times. Thank you for asking, Mathias."

He made her laugh as he pulled her onto his lap, and she went willingly. Straddling him, she felt his warmth envelope her. Running her fingers through his hair, she whispered, "And I never wore gloves once."

"Why didn't you tell me when I was making you do all that stuff?" His arms went around her, and his hands slid up her bare back under her shirt.

"I did not want to ruin your fun. You thought you were so clever." She ran her fingers down his neck. He was warm, and she couldn't stop touching him.

"I *was* clever," he argued, but his hands had found her sides, and his thumbs were caressing the underside of her breasts.

She laughed at him. "You are cute, Mathias. Have we talked enough yet?"

Her fingers were working the buttons of his shirt, opening it to reveal his bare skin underneath. Once it was completely undone, she smoothed her hands up his chest and over his shoulders, then back into his blond hair.

His hands tightened around her waist, pulling her closer to him. "Yes." His voice was husky as his mouth closed over hers in a kiss.

Tess smiled and broke the kiss. Pulling out of his strong, warm arms, she stood and held out her hand to him. Relief washed through her when he took it, and she led him into her bedroom.

Dropping his hand, she pulled off the T-shirt she had recently thrown on. Tossing it on the floor, she looked up at him and saw his eyes were on her breasts as he pushed his own shirt off his shoulders. His hands went to his belt as she slid out of the leggings and panties she wore.

When they were both naked, she watched him take her in as she looked over his body in return. He was amazingly toned and muscular for just a North Dakota farmer. And all she wanted to do was to touch him.

He was the first to reach out to her, as his fingers brushed lightly over the tattoo on her pelvis. Then his fingers wrapped behind her and grabbed her butt, pulling her to him. Once she was pressed against him, his lips found hers again.

Her hands roamed over his body on their own accord as her tongue slid into his mouth, and her kisses grew desperate. His hands moved up her body until they cupped her breasts, and he ran his thumbs over her sensitive nipples. She moaned at the sensations coursing through her body.

Turning, he sat down on the bed and moved her so that she was standing between his legs. His arms then went around her, and his lips found her nipple that was just level with his mouth.

She was still moaning as his hand slid down and cupped her core before his fingers expertly found her clit, making her call out his name as her hand fisted in his hair. She didn't want any of this to stop.

With her body so close to release, he rolled her onto the bed, taking her by surprise. She laughed and whispered hoarsely, "Tell a girl when you do that."

His response was to kiss her as he settled between her legs. Tess slid her fingers down his chest, then lower so she could caress his hard erection. Knowing he was as ready as she was, she whispered, "Please, now, please."

Again, he had no response to her words. So, she wrapped her legs around him, telling him with her body what she wanted since words were not working. It worked, and she groaned as he filled her slowly, too slowly, so she shifted her hips to take him in faster and deeper.

To her surprise, he grabbed her hips and held them in place, slowing her down. Tess grabbed the sheet below her to get traction, trying to break free from his hands and make him go faster. His lips were nuzzling her breast again as she moaned, "Faster, please, faster."

But he held back and was slowly sliding in and out, using his tongue to tease her nipples. Her body screamed for the release he was keeping from her. She slowly shook her head back and forth at the sensations he was sending through her body—she wanted more.

Finally, she let go of the sheets and grabbed his hands, pulling them away from her hips. Tess brought their joined hands over her head so that she could finally pick up the pace. Math closed his eyes and let out a slow breath. She could see his resolve breaking down, and almost immediately, he gave in and matched his rhythm with hers. Tess could feel herself spasming around him, groaning his name as she came. He soon followed, then rolled them onto their sides and caressed her spent body.

Once their breathing became even, and they were able to speak, he ran his hand down her side and touched her tattoo again. "I love when you can't even make words because of what I'm doing to you."

Tess sucked in a breath and flopped onto her back. She whispered to the ceiling, "Shit."

Sitting up, he looked down at her in confusion. "I thought that was a good thing?"

Running her hands over her face, she was glad the only light in the room came from the doorway to the living room because she was blushing from head to toe. Everything she had said had been in Russian. No wonder he didn't do anything she had asked him. Just like when she got mad, when she was having good sex, she had no time to translate before she spoke.

"It is a good thing; you make me forget how to speak." *English*, she didn't add as she smiled at him, hoping he wouldn't notice it was fake.

"I noticed it the other times. You were more talkative this time." He rolled over her again and kissed her.

Giving in to the kiss, she realized she would have to control her tongue when he was around. She did not want him to know about her past yet. She wasn't ready to share everything with him.

CHAPTER 18

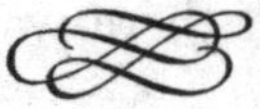

THE ALARM WENT off at 6:00 am. Tess groaned and shut it off, snuggling further into the warm covers. Math watched her as she did it, but then again, he had been watching her for almost an hour. But now, she was supposed to be awake, so he was able to slide his hand up her body. No need to worry about waking her.

At his touch, she sat completely upright, pulling the sheet close to her as she looked around. Her gray eyes were on him for a moment before she flopped back down beside him. She sighed, "Mathias."

"Did you forget I was here?" He ran a finger from her hairline to her chin.

She smiled at him. "For a moment. It has been a long time since I woke up with someone."

"I could tell. Sometimes you're jumpy," he said and then kissed the woman.

He had not wanted last night to end, but it had. Early. After leaving her at her door with barely a goodbye, he made it halfway home before slamming on the brakes and turning his truck back toward town. If nothing else, he wanted to kiss her just once. Again.

Their date had gone better than he had ever thought it was going to go. Convinced that they would be at all-out war by the time they made it to Grand Forks, he had been surprised that she was interesting and easy to talk to. Every word she said made him realize how wrong he had been about her. And she seemed interested in him as well.

His biggest issue with her was that she was very guarded when it came to her family and her past. She was okay with telling a story from her childhood now and again, but nothing too deep. Nothing too personal. He wondered if there was something she was hiding. This morning, he didn't care.

Cupping her butt, he pulled her body to his as he deepened the kiss. He was glad he came back. She felt as good against his body as she had last night. He had been nervous when he knocked on her door not ten minutes after dropping her off but was rewarded by her letting him in.

She pushed him out of her arms as her alarm went off again. Math tried to pull her back to him, but she squirmed away, giggling. "I have to get up. Work."

He brushed a finger over her breast, then followed it with his lips, asking, "When do you have to be at work?"

Her fingers went into his hair. "7:45 am."

"I think we have time. I'll be quick. I swear," he said as his hand glided down her body.

She made a noise he didn't recognize and pushed him away again. "I have to be ready by seven. I call my mother every morning at seven."

"Really quick?" He gently bit her nipple, making her groan.

"No, I should have set the alarm for earlier." She scrubbed her hands over her face as he continued with her breasts.

"You should have told me. I was up an hour ago. I would have woken you." Her body stilled under his.

"What did you do for an hour?" she whispered.

Pulling his eyes away from her glorious breast, he looked into her face as he replied, "I watched you sleep. You are beautiful when you sleep."

"But not when I am awake?" She couldn't suppress her grin at her teasing.

"You weren't awake when I was looking then. Now that you are, I can say that you're more beautiful when you are awake." He kissed her cheek, then placed more kisses across her jaw.

She laughed and pushed at him again. "I have to get up. Mama gets moody when I do not call."

Sitting up, she tossed the blankets away from her, and he was rewarded by getting to see her entire body less than an arm's length away from him. Reaching out, he ran his hand down her back, then around her waist, and pulled her back into his body. "You can't leave."

"Mathias, stop. If you are interested, I have to take a shower. I believe there is enough room for two in there." Instantly, he let her go and rolled out of bed. "But you have to promise I will be ready for work at 7:00 am."

Walking around the bed to the side she was on, he held out his hand and said, "I promise." Then he pulled her to her feet. Then he quickly wrapped his arms around her and all but ran her to the bathroom. From the sound she made as they went, he couldn't tell if she was mad or happy. When she raked her hands down his back, he knew she was as excited as he was about a hot shower. A *very* hot shower.

SOME PROMISES WERE MEANT to be broken, but she was ready and showing him out the door at 7:05 am, so he felt it was a success. Neither talked about seeing the other again, but there was no way he would not see her again. By the way she kissed him at the door, she wanted to see him again as well. He was starting to realize that neither one of them was very good at dating.

On his drive home, he wondered if she was telling her mom about him. Maybe she already had; she talked to the woman every morning. She lived nine hours from her family, but she talked to them more often than he did his, and they were just down the road.

Flashing blue lights in his mirror had him cursing as he pulled over. Forgetting about the woman who was consuming his thoughts, he looked at the dash of his truck. Had he been speeding? Have a taillight out? What had he done wrong? Sure, he was not paying a lot of attention to driving this morning, but he had been driving on this road his entire life.

Rolling his window down, he looked in the mirror to see which cop had pulled him over. There was only a handful of police in town, and he knew them all. But the one walking toward him was his favorite. Hue Strong had been his best friend since they started kindergarten together.

"Mr. Nordskov, do you know why I am pulling you over this fine morning?" Hue asked, tapping the notepad he carried. Hue hadn't been back in Landstad for long, close to a year, but he had been raised here and knew everyone and everything.

"I don't. I wasn't speeding."

"You're right; this is not a speed issue. I stopped you this morning to issue you a parking ticket," Hue said, opening his notepad before pushing up his hat to reveal more of his short red hair.

"What are you talking about? I was driving," Math argued. "You can't get a parking ticket for driving."

"But your pickup spent the entire night on Main Street. The entire night, Mr. Nordskov. What were you doing on Main Street?" Hue leaned against Math's pickup.

"None of your business," Math replied to his friend, who happened to live across from Tess. This Main Street crew was an odd group.

"I think it has to do with a certain bank president, one who a certain Mr. Nordskov was just—not a few months ago—wanting to run out of this town on rails." Hue had gotten an earful since January about his anger about Tess.

"I might have changed my mind about that," Math said sheepishly.

"Oh, I can see that. Or I did when I was patrolling last night." Hue laughed as he opened his pad and started to write.

"There are no laws against parking on Main Street all night," Math answered as he watched his friend writing on his pad.

"I am not writing you a ticket. I'm making you a list of people who get to tell you 'Told you so.' Because we all told you how nice she was, and you were being an idiot." Hue laughed and handed him the paper.

With that, he went back to his patrol car and left. Math looked at the list Hue had written. Hue, Amanda, Mia. Just three surprised him. Looking at the list, he wondered why his friend had written his sister's name as Amanda, not Mandy like everyone called her. Hue called her that. But suddenly it was Amanda.

Smiling, he crumpled the paper and threw it in the passenger seat. He would have to keep an eye on Hue and Mandy. Not that he would be able to see much since they lived across the hall from each other, and he was miles away from them.

But first, he had to get home and get into the field. Maybe he would find time to call Tess this afternoon. Or at least text.

CHAPTER 19

THE MORNING SUN was warm against her skin, even if the air held a bit of April morning chill in it. Tess was leaning against the back wall of the bank next to the rear exit. Again, she needed fresh air on her lunch break, but today she had called her sister instead of going to the café.

This morning's half an hour phone call with her mama had left her on edge. The older woman hadn't spoken once about her papa. Not one word. Their talks were usually peppered with mentions of the man who dominated her mama's life. Today nothing.

Tess chickened out on asking Ilya about their Dad and what might be going on. Instead, Tess had finally told her the news. To her surprise, the woman hadn't even said, "Oh, Terezilya," in her disappointed voice—she was too excited to be disappointed.

Instead, she had said, "See, Terezilya? You are too young for menopause. And we do not get cancer." As if her family was so special.

"You were right. I just could not see the obvious answer. Tasha realized it before me," Tess said with a smile.

"Natasha would; she has the eye. But you do too. Are you coming home to have it? Are you seeing a doctor there?" Ilya asked.

Sitting up straighter, Tess ignored her sister's questions. No way was she rushing nine hours in labor to have a baby. Instead, she asked,

"Did you ever have any problems? Being pregnant or in delivery? We never talked about that."

"Oh, now and again. My Terri and Anya were both born breech, and I had the miscarriage," Ilya stated as if those were everyday occurrences and not medical issues.

"Wait, I didn't know that. Let me get to my office so that I can write this down," she said, going back into the bank and shutting her office door behind her. By the time she had hung up on her sister, she had written Ilya's complete medical history and most of their mom's from what Ilya could remember. It was enough to scare Tess stiff.

Her mother's history. Being the youngest, she never saw her mom pregnant, so it was easy to forget she ever had been. Sure, her six children were around all the time, but Tess had never questioned the gaps in age between the children. Sergey and Ilya were eight years apart, and so were Ilya and her. The fact that there were pregnancies in those gaps had Tess worrying about everything.

Over the years, she had heard about the four children of her parents that never made it out of Russia. All had died before the age of ten, including Terezilya the first, who had died the fall before Tess herself was born. But she had not heard so much about the stillborn babies or the miscarriages. Now she realized that she could lose the baby, that there was a high possibility of that happening.

There was no way she was telling Mathias only then to lose her baby and lose the job that would take her closer to her family. Though she hadn't heard back, she figured she would soon.

Tapping her pen on her desk, she remembered that Mandy had worked with high-risk pregnancies and babies with medical issues before moving back to Landstad. Mandy would be able to tell her if she was worrying for nothing, or she'd send her to a doctor who could save her baby. If that were possible.

Picking up her phone, she called a Nordskov, a different one from the day before. She was surprised when Mandy answered the phone at the clinic. She was usually too busy, and messages had to be left. Or at least that is what Tess had heard since she had never been to the clinic herself.

"Mandy, do you have a few minutes to talk to me today?"

"If you can come right in, my 11:00 am canceled," Mandy said. It was a few minutes past that time.

"Yes." She hung up before she chickened out.

On her way out of the bank, she told Beatrice at the reception desk she was going out for lunch again. Then she walked down the block, taking a deep breath as she pushed her way into the clinic, glad the trip wasn't long enough for her to chicken out.

Mandy was sitting at the desk and was fiddling with the computer and some papers. There were no chairs sitting in front of the desk, so Tess stood, not wanting to move in a chair.

"I can tell something is wrong, Tess. What is it? Did you talk to Math?" Mandy asked about her brother.

"Yes, thank you for his number yesterday."

"Do you want to talk here or back in the exam room?" Mandy gestured at the exam room behind her. Before Tess could answer Mandy stood up and led her down the hallway.

Once in the room, Tess finally sat, but it didn't make her feel better. She just felt Mandy was going to tell her she would probably lose the baby.

Mandy turned on the computer in that room and asked, "Tess, what is it then?"

Tess took a deep breath and said, "I am pregnant, and I talked to my sister. She said her pregnancies were great. Then we talked about my mother's, which were not so great."

"Did you talk to your mom?" Mandy asked, not questioning her at all about the pregnancy or how she got that way or even who the dad is. That made Tess relax a little.

"No, I haven't told her yet. And she is older now, and I don't like to worry her." Tess wasn't sure how her mother would take the news of her pregnancy yet. She was afraid of disappointing her parents again.

"Can you tell me about it? You know I cannot tell anyone, right? *Anyone*." Mandy emphasized the last word.

Tess knew Mandy thought the baby was her brother's, which is why Tess hadn't planned to come over here and see his sister for this. Well, she hadn't thought about seeing anyone yet.

"I have it on paper. I wrote it down; it was easier." Tess pulled out a paper labeled Mama and handed it to her friend.

Mandy spent a few minutes looking it over. "You should have been a doctor, Tess. Your writing is awful."

Tess laughed at the back-handed compliment. It wasn't the first time she had been told that. "I am a lefty. I write fast but not properly."

"Can I ask what some of this means?" Mandy set the paper on the desk.

"Yes, each line is a child and what we think happened, but some may not be right."

"So, this one was a girl, baby number four, stillborn?" Mandy asked.

"Yes."

"So, each line is a child?" Mandy pointed at a line.

"Yes."

She looked up at Tess. "Which one is you?"

"Second to the last." Tess pointed at her line; all it said was girl.

How old was your mother when you were born?" Mandy leaned back after reading the short line.

"Forty-two." Tess knew that answer before the phone call with her sister; it was a well-known fact in the family.

"How about the last one?" Mandy looked at the paper again.

"Forty-three." Tess smiled, though she didn't know why.

"The final one was stillborn. Do you know why?"

"No, she would never have said if she knew. Ilya did not know either," Tess replied, worrying what Mandy was asking about.

"Ilya?" Mandy asked.

"My sister."

"Which line is she?" Mandy again looked at the paper.

Tess looked at the paper and pointed. "This one. She is my only sister."

"How were her pregnancies?" Mandy questioned before adding, "No, you said hers were great. No miscarriages or stillbirths?"

Tess didn't open the file and hand over that paper. She wanted to focus more on her mother's past since that was closer to her future. "Just one, when she was in her twenties."

"Was it her first, second, last?" Mandy took out her pen and started to write on Tess's paper.

"No," was all Tess said as Mandy's black pen wrote on her blue-inked paper.

Mandy looked up at her. "Which birth then?"

"Sorry," she said and opened her file and looked. "Fifth pregnancy."

"I have some questions. You only have one sister? But this one was a live birth girl a few years before your sister's birth."

Tess looked. "Yes, she died before I was born."

"How?" Mandy wrote something on the paper.

"Measles."

"How?"

"I do not know, the usual way you die of measles. I never really heard. I was not there," Tess said, looking at Mandy, who should know how a person dies of such diseases.

"How many others died of something after the age of, say, a week?" Mandy asked.

Tess leaned over and pointed, and Mandy marked them also. "These two also died of measles, and this one of mumps. These two died after I was born, but I do not remember them."

"How many are alive today? Total?" Mandy picked up the paper and looked at it.

Tess closed her eyes. "Six." Then she opened them to watch her friend.

Mandy was silent as they looked over the paper and then looked over Tess. "Are you feeling well?"

"Yes, I am fine. No symptoms at all. That is why I did not realize I was pregnant for so long."

"How long?" Mandy turned to the computer and started typing.

"Since February. Am I going to lose her, Mandy? Is it bad?" Tess asked point-blank.

"I don't know, Tess. I have a friend I want to send you to. I'm concerned about your mom's history. You were right to be nervous about it. It's not good. The promising thing is your sister seems to have a good history; one miscarriage and four live births is promising," Mandy said, looking at the paper again.

"Twelve," Tess replied, looking at the paper with all its marks.

"Twelve what?" Mandy looked at her.

"Ilya had twelve babies, not four," Tess said, pointing to her on the list.

Mandy raised an eyebrow in surprise. "Your sister has twelve children?"

"Of her own, yes. Her second husband had six when they married, so she claims eighteen." Tess looked over the paper.

"With no issues?" Mandy picked up her pen again.

Tess shrugged. "Oh, I'm sure it was not as rosy as she always made it out to be, but she made it look like it was nothing."

"No, I mean she only had one miscarriage in thirteen pregnancies?" Mandy restated.

"Sorry, yes, just the one." Tess bit her lip.

"I'm starting to not worry," Mandy said and leaned back in her chair.

"Because of my sister?"

"That's right. If she had no issues, then maybe you will follow her and not your mother's path. Can I get your information in the system?"

Tess nodded, but she was already in the system since it was tied to the one in Grand Forks where she usually went to the doctor.

Mandy's eyes went to the screen. "Have you ever been pregnant before? I should have asked right away."

"No, never," Tess answered, watching her read.

"You were not born in this country." Mandy pointed at something on the screen.

"That is correct."

"When did you move here?"

"When I was eight."

Mandy grinned and turned back to her. "You don't even have an accent. I am now completely fascinated by you."

"What?"

"You are a bank president, and you were not even born in this country. And you're going to have my brother's baby. Does he know?" Mandy leaned forward.

"That I am a bank president, yes. Not the rest of it." She admitted that it was Mathias's baby, wondering if his sister would keep her secret if she never told him. Suddenly, she wished she had just gone to Grand Forks for this appointment instead of dragging Mandy in the middle of it.

"We have got to do some Russian serial killers for book club. You'd be able to pronounce all their names and the city names. It will be amazing. You can speak Russian, right?" Mandy leaned forward.

"Yes, I speak Russian still." Tess smiled at her excitement. Very few people she had met actually thought it was interesting that she was born there.

"Dang it." Mandy slapped her hand against the table. "I can't tell anyone."

"Sorry, you cannot." Tess grinned at her friend.

"And I bet you are not going to either." Mandy sighed.

"It is not something I bring up, and nobody else does either," Tess said in way of reply.

"Let's get this exam done then. How much are we doing today?" Mandy asked, a little disappointed that she would have to keep Tess's secret.

"Can we just do the test today? Then you can tell me if I have to go see your doctor friend."

"I don't think you'll need to see a specialist. Your sister's history will align with yours better. I really don't think this is a big deal." Mandy held up the heavily marked paper.

After the tests confirmed what she already knew, Tess was glad she had gone to Mandy instead of anyone else. It had been a little awkward at first, but Mandy was good at putting people at ease. As

Tess was leaving the office with her positive result, Mandy stopped her with a hand on her arm. "Are you going to tell Math?"

"I do not know. We do not always get along. I know you are his sister, but he and I sometimes do not mix," Tess said.

"You seem to have mixed once. Maybe you could again." Mandy chuckled.

"You saw him at Easter, Mandy," she reminded her.

"Yes, I did, more than you did. He couldn't keep his eyes off you. And Mom said he asked about you after we left," Mandy replied.

"I have applied for another job in another town," Tess admitted and then added, "If I take it, I will not be telling Mathias. The job will let me be closer to my family."

Mandy's smile fell. "I see."

"I have to think about the baby. I want her to know my family, my heritage," Tess explained, hoping that Mandy would understand.

"What about him?"

"I do not even know if he wants to be a part of this."

"I know him, Tess. There's no way he would not be a part of his child's life."

"I just do not know yet."

Saying goodbye, Tess headed to work with at least one answer she needed before making her decision about the new job. She was definitely pregnant, and Mandy had assured her she would stay that way. But the Mathias thing was still in the air. She would do what was right for her baby, whatever that was.

CHAPTER 20

MATHIAS'S TEXTS throughout the afternoon distracted Tess in a good way. Finally, she had been able to concentrate on work, mostly. She was still worried about her dad but far less worried about her baby.

She had received the first text from Math just after she got back from the clinic, and she happily texted him back. The texts had been about nothing, just little comments about his day or asking about hers. But she enjoyed them. They lifted her spirits when the feeling of impending doom was hanging over her.

She didn't text him about her concerns over her family. Those two worlds had always been easy to keep separate, but with Mathias in the picture, they were starting to butt up against one another. The baby made them overlap, and she wasn't prepared for that just yet.

By mid-afternoon, she had received a call from the other bank—the job was hers if she wanted it, and they would give her a week to decide whether she would take it. Now she knew she had to make a decision. By then, she would have to get the nerve up to tell Mathias about the baby. After yesterday, she saw that they could maybe make something work, and it could be amazing. She could easily fall for him, stay with him.

But the dream had reminded her that if she chose to stay, she chose this life and would have to leave her past behind. Was she ready to walk away from the family she loved? To not go back again? For years, she had known that she could stop going home, and the connection she had with them would easily be severed. After all, no one ever came to visit her.

There would still be calls and texts, and she would remain close to Tasha and Ilya, but once her parents were gone, she would have little reason to stay connected with anyone else. Her brothers didn't really call, only Mike every once in a while, but that was about their parents.

Tossing her phone on her desk after sending another text to Math, she looked out her window at the alley behind the bank. After yesterday's date, she realized that her original choice between Mathias being a dad to her baby or not had evolved. Now she knew that if she stayed, she would have to shut the door on her past, on her heritage. If she chose Mathias, she chose a new life, an American life.

But at least her baby would understand her if she was an American. No more back and forth, living on the edge of two worlds. She would be fully in one world. Her baby couldn't live in the balance as Tess had for years. Her baby needed to be born *in* the world, not on the edge of it. She deserved that.

If she hadn't left work early the day before, she would have gone home to her apartment today. She had actually put herself into a depression about it. Shoving the emotions down, she forced herself to work; she had things piling up on her desk. Close to 4:00 pm, she got another text from Mathias.

Math: Do you want to come out for supper? The kids will be here.

Looking at the text, she wondered what it meant. Did he want her to meet his kids? He must; the text said he did. Without overthinking it, she typed,

Tess: Yes.

So now she was going to meet his kids, her baby's siblings. They would be the names her baby would talk about all the time if she told Mathias about her.

After her dream, Tess knew the baby was a girl. Since the day she realized she was pregnant, she had thought it was a girl, felt it was a girl. But after the dream, she knew it was a girl. Her daughter.

By 5:00 pm, when she was locking the bank for the night, she was about ready to text Mathias to say she wasn't going out there. But she needed a distraction, and a bunch of kids was perfect for that. After changing into jeans and a pink blouse in an attempt to raise her spirits, she headed out to his farm.

On the way, she called Tasha. "Hi Tasha, it is Tess."

"Hi, Tessy! I can only talk for a second; supper is almost ready," Tasha stated, sounding busy.

"Is there something going on with my papa?" No need to hedge with Tasha. They knew each other too well for that.

"Well, how much do you know?" She could tell Tasha stopped whatever she was doing.

"Nothing, just that Mama didn't sound right this week. She didn't talk about Papa like usual. What is happening there?" Tess demanded, her heart in her throat. Something was wrong with her dad.

"Something happened after you left at Easter. He was in the hospital for a day. Mike got him out, and he has gotten much better," Tasha admitted.

"What kind of something?" Tess needed to know. She suddenly wanted to drive the nine hours to be with her mom and dad.

"Heart something. They did not tell me everything. Mike might not even really know. He doesn't understand as much English as he likes to think he does."

"When were they going to tell me? Ever?" Tess asked again as she stopped just after turning into Mathias's driveway. Throwing on the parking brake, she got out of the car to pace.

"I don't know. Maybe when they knew more," Tasha offered.

"Why didn't anyone tell me when he was hospitalized?" Tess pushed, knowing Tasha was not part of the decision to not tell her.

"I wasn't there," Tasha defended herself.

"But you knew. You could have called me," Tess said, leaning against the car and closing her eyes.

"I know. I just felt…." She stopped talking.

"I feel like I am not a part of the family anymore," she whispered. She knew she had switched to speaking in Russian, but she didn't know when it had happened.

"Your too far away, Tessy." Tasha didn't say anything Tess didn't already know herself.

"Should I walk away from them, Tasha?" The words slipped out. Tess needed her best friend to say it, so she knew it was what she needed to do.

"That's not what I said. We are your family." Tasha said through tears.

"Thank you, Tasha," Tess whispered as she hung up on her niece despite her trying to say something else as the call ended.

Her dad was failing, she was nine hours away, and nobody was telling her about it. Would they even call when he was dead? Would they hide that from her? What else have they been hiding from her?

Tess picked up her phone to call Ilya to ask about their dad, but she saw Mathias walking down the driveway toward her. There was no time to make the call, so she tossed her phone back in her car through the open window and closed her eyes.

Images of her father rushed through her mind—when she was young, and he was already middle-aged, and now when he was old. To her, he was never a young man; she had never even seen pictures from before they came to America. In her mind, she heard him shaking his head in disappointment, saying, "Terezilya, you know better." How many times had he said that to her?

Tess took a few deep breaths, wiping the tears away before Mathias could see them. She could cry when she was alone, not in front of people. Once she got home, she could call Ilya, maybe on the way.

"Are you scared?" Math teased as he approached her.

"Nothing scares me," Tess said, trying to sound normal, trying not to think about how scared she was of losing her dad.

"What's wrong? Have you been crying?" He pulled her into his arms and hugged her once he reached her.

"No, I have not," she argued, resting her head on his shoulder. She needed to be held, and he calmed her just by holding her.

"If you need to keep *not* crying, go ahead." He tightened his hold on her and rocked her gently for a long time.

Finally, she was able to get her emotions under control and stuffed her memories back in her past where they belonged. Pushing away from him, she said, "I am fine now. Thank you."

Math released her from the hug but held on to her hand. "Are you sure you're okay?"

"Yes, just a bad day at work," she whispered her lie.

"I really don't think so. Tess Thorn doesn't let things at the bank make her sad. Is it your family?" His blue eyes pierced hers. How had he figured it out so quickly?

"I do not want to talk about it," she whispered again.

"Okay, I'll let it go. For now." He kissed her cheek.

"Thank you." She tried to compose herself again. It was all too much. She should have stayed home today.

"Let's walk to the house. I'll have Cora drive your baby up," he said, pulling her away from her car.

"She is only fifteen! She cannot drive yet," Tess argued as she followed him reluctantly. But he was still holding her hand, so she went.

"She can drive it down the driveway. If she crashes it, I'll buy you a new one." He squeezed her hand. "She's mad that I invited my girl-friend, as she calls you, to have a meal with us."

"I am sorry I am causing tension between you and your daughter." She looked out at the field along the driveway. It was still black with nothing growing yet.

"You are not causing anything. She's always mad at me for something."

"You love your children a lot," she replied, knowing he would love their baby just as much as the three he already had. She then realized she couldn't deprive him of a child to love.

"Everybody loves their children, but I do enjoy mine a lot. I wouldn't trade any of them for anything." He was walking slowly, letting her get her emotions together.

"I know." The big farmhouse was just across the yard from them. Mathias's house, home. Is this what her daughters future would be like? Dropping her baby off here to visit her father? Would she get a bedroom here? Tess knew she would; she would get everything she ever wanted here. Her baby's life would never mirror her own. Her baby would have clothes, toys, and food. Her baby would never know what it feels like to not have anything. It would all be right here.

"If you don't want to meet them today, you don't have to." He must have felt her tense up.

"No, my thoughts are too much today. I need a distraction," she admitted as she noticed a teenager on the porch, watching them. The girl who looked so much like her father was pretending to be on her phone as she leaned against the porch railing until they got closer.

"Did your girlfriend finally show up?" the teenager yelled at her dad as they approached the house.

Once they were close enough for normal conversation, Math replied, "Hailey, this is Tess Thorn. Tess, my daughter, Hailey."

Tess looked from father to daughter again. Without a doubt, this was his daughter. The teenager looked just like Mandy, only younger. What puzzled Tess was that Mathias hadn't corrected Hailey. But what was he to her?

"Hello, Hailey. Your dad says good things about you. He is very proud of you," she said to the teenager, who barely looked up from her phone.

"He hasn't said much about you," Cora stated flatly.

"*Hailey,*" Math warned.

"He probably does not. I do not talk much about him either," Tess said because it was true. So far, she hadn't told many people about him. And by many, she meant nobody but Tasha.

"Do you have kids?" the teen asked.

"No, not yet." Tess was getting used to the idea of her baby still.

Just then, the door behind them slammed open, and a boy of

around eleven came out. He seemed to not be paying much attention to what was going on around him and stopped when he saw his dad and her. Tess didn't hold his attention long before he asked, "Dad, when is supper?"

Math smiled at his son and said, "Mason, this is Tess Thorn."

"Dad's girlfriend," Cora provided.

The boy looked Tess from head to toe. "You're kind of old to be Dad's girlfriend."

"Mason," Math warned his son.

"But she is so much older than Jason's dad's girlfriend. I thought when old guys got girlfriends, they were younger than she is," Mason argued his point.

"I understand, Mason. When we met, I guess I forgot to tell him I was older. Maybe he didn't notice," she joked.

"He doesn't always pay attention," the boy agreed, looking at his dad.

"How old are you?" Cora asked, looking her up and down also. It seemed having the girl warm up to her was going to take time. A lot of time.

"How old are you?" Tess turned the question around on the girl, the way she usually did when someone asked her age. She'd learned the trick years before. Usually, people forget they asked if she countered with a question.

"Fifteen, almost sixteen," the teen stated proudly.

"When you are twenty-two, I will be twice your age. How old am I?" Tess smiled at her. *See how fast she can get it, or if she even tries.*

"Thirty-seven," Mason provided from behind his sister.

"I was getting there, Mason," Cora said angrily at her brother.

Tess grinned at the boy. "Good job, Mason."

"Okay, I have to get supper ready. You two go and get Tess's car from the end of the driveway. Don't hit anything. Call if you have any trouble," Math said to his older kids. Both looked at their dad for a second and then took off, happy to get to drive a car. Alone.

"You did not tell them how to drive a stick shift," she said as she watched them go.

He pulled her into his arms and kissed her. "I get more alone time with you, and they will call before coming back."

Laughing at his tactics, she asked, "What about the third one?"

"She's in the house." He nuzzled her neck.

"If she looks just like all of you but shorter and cuter, she is watching from behind the door." She waved at the little girl looking down at them.

Groaning, he lifted his head to look at the blond watching them. "Come out here, Juniper."

The girl did as requested and came out of the house, but she lingered by the door. Tess went up the steps and crouched down in front of the eight-year-old. "Do you remember me, Juniper?"

The little girl nodded. "You are Mia's friend."

"Yes, I am. We met at Easter," Tess reminded her of their meeting place, in case the girl couldn't remember.

"I know, you have two middle names," she pointed out.

"I do." Tess smiled and was glad the girl had remembered her.

"I only have one," Juniper confessed.

"Your name is Juniper. I love that name." She ran her hand over the girl's long blonde hair.

"It's long. I have to write it all the time."

"I have a long name too, so I understand." Tess thought she had the kids beat for long name with Terezilya Aleksandrov.

"Tess isn't long," Juniper insisted.

She winked. "Tess is not my real name."

"What is your real name?" The girl's familiar blue eyes were wide with wonder.

Glancing at Mathias, who was watching her closely, she whispered in the girl's ear, "Terezilya."

"I have never heard that name before," the little girl whispered.

"Do not tell anyone. I do not want them to know. I like being called Tess, but if you want, my niece calls me Tessy," Tess replied, knowing the little girl would never get her tongue around the Russian name.

"Can I call you Tessy too?" Juniper asked.

"Only if I can sometimes call you Junebug," Tess answered with a smile.

"Only once in a while. Tessy," she tried out the name.

"Okay, Junebug," she said, making the little girl giggled.

After talking to the kids, she felt better, less like she was falling. Less like her life was suddenly out of control. Without thinking, she hugged the little girl who might look exactly like the daughter she would have one day. Juniper hugged her back, and Tess felt even better about the future.

"Where is Hailey?" Juniper asked when Tess let her go.

"At the end of the driveway, getting Tess's car," Math said.

The girl looked excited. "Can I go see?"

"Sure, just watch out for the car on the way and stay off the road," Math called out as the girl headed across the yard like the older two had a few minutes before.

"You have good kids, Mathias." She sat down against the door when her knees wouldn't just push her back to her feet anymore. The joys of getting old.

"They are, but you're great with kids." He walked up to her and held out his hand to help her up.

"I should be. I have been around them my entire life. Kids, kids, kids … they are everywhere." He pulled her to her feet and into his arms again. He was pretty good at getting her back into his arms.

With his arms around her, he held her close and said, "So the oldest is forty-three. How old is the youngest?" he asked about her nieces and nephews she assumed.

Closing her eyes and letting herself just let go, she said, "Six."

"I mean your nieces and nephews, not *their* kids." He ran his fingers through her hair.

"Ilya's youngest is six. Her name is Zsophia, and she will only answer to that. Not Zsophie, Just Zsophia," she said quietly, thinking about the little girl.

"You say it different. Does it start with a Z or an S?" he asked while rocking her again gently.

Sighing, she rested her head on his shoulder, "Yes, both."

He must have let it go because he didn't say anything, just held her. This was the most hugging she had done in years. It was a day she needed them the most, though. Could Mathias feel it? She was starting to think he could read her thoughts, even if he couldn't speak the language that usually bounced around in her mind.

CHAPTER 21

Burgers were eaten, and dishes had been done, and Tess was still quiet. Not that she hadn't interacted with his kids like she had known them her entire life and knew just what to say to them. Because she had, but it seemed her mind had been elsewhere most of the evening.

When the kids had finally given up on getting the car started, Tess had walked down there to help since Math was making supper. When they had returned, all had been laughing, and Cora had been driving the old red car. Once in the car they decided to take a longer drive and went around the mile section.

Cora had been so excited that she got to drive that she had forgotten she was mad at the world when they got back. The teen had also found herself a new friend in the woman she called "his girl-friend." Math had liked the sound of it.

During the fifteen-minute drive, Tess had won over all the children. Once back, they were friendly and helpful to the woman. They didn't even comment too much about her eating a burger with her usual knife and fork or even that she didn't finish everything on her plate. After the meal, the kids had invited her to watch a movie with them, and Math let her go while he cleaned the kitchen.

Now he was sitting next to her on the couch watching a movie, but he could tell she wasn't interested in what the kids had picked. She was just there for them. He liked her even more, knowing that she was doing this for his kids, even if she was uninterested.

Cora got up and said, "Anyone want something to drink?"

Math looked at his daughter, confused. She had never cared about anyone else's needs before. They all said yes, and she went out to the kitchen. Within a few minutes, she asked, "Dad, where's the pop you just bought?"

"In the pantry," he answered from his spot.

"I can't see it," she said from the doorway.

"I'll get it." Math huffed but got up. He just wanted to watch a movie with Tess, even if she didn't want to see it.

Once in the kitchen, he went into the pantry, but the pop was gone. In confusion, he walked back into the kitchen and saw it on the counter. Cora was next to it.

"It's right there." He pointed to it.

"I know, you idiot. I want to talk to you," Cora said quietly.

"To me?" he asked, once again confused. His daughter usually hated talking with him. Most of the time, she didn't talk to him at all.

"Yes, it's about Tess."

"I thought you didn't like her?" He hadn't expected her to like Tess so quickly.

"It's not that. When we were in her car, her phone was in there." Cora looked at the doorway to the living room.

"Did you look at her phone?" he accused.

"Yes and no. We wouldn't have, but she got like a thousand texts. And a dozen calls."

"I think maybe not that many." He chuckled at her exaggeration.

"No, Dad, really. At least ten calls, and the texts didn't stop. When she got in the car to help me, she didn't look at it; she shut it off. She hasn't turned it on.

"It's none of our business, Hailey. It's her phone, which means her business. Not ours."

"They were from a guy, Dad."

"Hailey," he warned.

"A guy kept saying, 'Sorry, I didn't mean it that way.' Stuff like that. Does she have a boyfriend, Dad?"

"What was the guy's name?" Was his daughter actually trying to protect him? Was this the same daughter who barely talked to him week after week, and when she did, it was to tell him to stay out of her life?

"Nat."

"That's her friend, a female friend." His heart hurt for Tess. Something happened between her and her niece, and it had really bothered her. So much so, it made her cry earlier. Not in front of him, but she hadn't hid it well enough for him not to notice.

"Are you sure?"

"Yes, she's her niece. They are very close." Or were, he didn't know now.

"The texts made me wonder." Cora shrugged.

"Hailey, all I know is that something happened on a call just as she was getting here. That's why we left her car. It was something with her family, but she won't talk about it," he admitted to his daughter. He wouldn't push her about it, either. She had to want to tell him.

His daughter let it drop, and they brought the drinks into the living room for everyone. Sitting back down, he pulled Tess closer into his arms. Her body was stiff, but then she melted into him and sighed. Neither of them touched their drinks, he just held her in the semi-darkness, and she held him tight. Her eyes were on the screen, but he could tell her mind was elsewhere.

When the credits rolled, she announced that she had to get home. Not wanting to push her, he just followed her through the house and out to her car. As they left, he told the kids it was time to get ready for bed and that he would be up in a bit to make sure they were doing it. Tonight would have been a good night for his ex to have them. It was hard to parent while Tess was hurting.

At her car, she turned and looked at him. "I had a good time tonight, Mathias. Your kids are great. You are a great dad."

"I think you won them over. But who couldn't like you?" he pulled her to him and brushed a kiss to her forehead.

"You on a good day."

"I don't know what I was even thinking then. Might be why I had sex with you on your birthday." He kissed her cheek, lingering as he took in her fresh smell for an extra moment.

She bit her lip and said, "I have to go."

"Stay," he whispered as his lips touched hers.

"I cannot. The children," she protested, but it wasn't a very strong argument.

"They will never know." He touched her lips again. "I don't want you to be alone. I know you won't talk to me about it, and I won't ask. But I want to be there for you."

To his surprise, she agreed to stay and let him lead her from her car and back into the house. In the kitchen, he told her how to get to his bedroom and then went up to make sure the kids were getting ready. All three were in their rooms, but Cora was talking on her phone. Leaving her alone, he got the other two to bed.

Once Mason was in bed reading, he went to Juniper's bedroom to read her a story, like he did every night. But he couldn't concentrate on the story. When he was almost done, his phone rang.

Sliding out of bed, he looked at the number. He didn't recognize it but decided to answer anyway. After he identified himself, he heard a voice ask, "Mr. Nordskov, I am looking for Tess Thorn. I talked to your sister at the clinic, Amanda. She is Tess's friend. She said Tessy might be there."

"Who is this?" he asked, but he already had a good idea. This had to be Tasha.

"Natasha Aleksandrov. Tessy is my aunt. Is she there? I cannot get her on her phone." Her voice had so much concern with a hint of an accent that had been very pronounced when she had said her name.

"Hello, Natasha. Tess is here, but I don't know if she wants to talk to you. She turned her phone off." Math didn't know if Tess would speak to the concerned woman.

"Please, Mr. Nordskov, I need to speak to her. I said something, and it was the wrong time," she pleaded.

"Yes, it really hurt her." Math kissed Juniper's head and left his daughter's room.

"I know. It had to be said, but not today. Not this week. We should have talked about it when she was here, before." The woman was crying now. His heart broke for the two friends who were so far apart.

"I'll see if she wants to talk. Hold on a moment." He put the phone to his chest as he looked around the house for Tess. He even checked outside to make sure her car was there. It was. Checking his bedroom, he saw her lying in a ball on the side of the bed. Her eyes were still open, and she was looking at the wall.

Sitting on the bed, he said, "Tasha called Mandy to get my number. She wants to talk."

Her eyes looked at him in confusion, making him wondered if she even understood what he said. Sitting up, she pulled her phone to her and turned it on. Then she said, "Hang up. I will call her."

Watching her scroll through her phone, he hung up on the woman who was probably still crying. With her phone to her ear, she was all business when she talked to her niece. "Tasha, this is Tess." He almost thought she would say from the bank with the tone she was using.

He slipped out of the room to give her some privacy, but not before hearing her say crisply, "No, Natasha, what you said earlier is what you meant. I do not belong."

Heading back to the check on the kids and let her have privacy, he wondered what she didn't belong to anymore. What was suddenly happening in her life that they would not approve of? Since Juniper was asleep, he checked on Mason, who was also asleep. Only Cora was still awake, so Math told her to get off her phone and go to bed. Her only answer was an eye roll.

Walking past his room, he heard that Tess was still on the phone. He left her to fix what was broken between the friends, but he heard something about a church. As he walked into the living room and sat on the couch, he wondered if she was having difficulties with her family because of him. He was of a different religion, and some people had a hard time with that. Maybe her parents did.

Based on everything she had said about them, they were older. But they had barely been together, so how could her parents be against them being together already? Math sat there, stewing over the idea that her parents could hate him and not even know him. What had he done? He really liked her. In fact, he could see them together after these last two days. He wanted them together.

Tonight, he hadn't wanted her to ever leave. She was the person everyone told him she was: nice and fun and perfect for him. There was still plenty he didn't know about her, but given time, she would trust him.

After an hour of wondering what was going on with her, he got up to check and see if she was still on the phone. But when he got to his room, the light was off, and she was under the covers, her phone on the table beside her. He was a little hurt she hadn't come out to find him.

Shedding his clothes, he climbed in with her and gathered her into his arms. He didn't think she was sleeping, but she pretended, so he let her. She was in his arms, and that was all that mattered.

CHAPTER 22

THE SUN HADN'T STARTED to rise yet when Tess slipped out of Mathias's warm and cozy bed. So far, she hadn't slept, and she wasn't going to now. Quietly she changed from the T-shirt she had borrowed into her clothes and slipped out of the house.

She was home before the firsts light of dawn illuminated her apartment. The talk with Tasha had helped her greatly, but not in the way she had thought it would. Tasha managed to convince Tess of something she should have known the entire time: she was staying in Landstad. This was her home now—her baby made this home. Tess couldn't take her baby from her father.

Even if she took the job and moved closer to her family, she would still not belong there. No matter how close or far she was from them, she could never be like her sister or her niece. Tess had a career, an education, and a life away from the immediate family. When she had the baby, she knew she would never quit her job and stay home with her; she would put the baby in daycare.

The baby would possibly say a few words of Russian but would not be able to talk with her grandma. By the time her daughter could talk to Tess's mom, she would be well over eighty. And they would only have a few visits a year, a few days each time. Not enough for either to know the other well. It was how it had to be.

Showering to clear the tears for work, she went to the bank early to get some work done before her employees showed up. Tess sat at her desk in the dark. The air conditioning had been left on overnight, so the place was chilly. Grabbing the name badge at the end of the desk, she turned it over and looked at her name: Tess Thorn, President.

That was something Terezilya Aleksandrov had dreamed of but would never have achieved. Every change had led her to this office. Did she want to go to a bigger bank? Yes. But she would stay here for the baby. This would be her home.

Tess picked up her phone and dialed her mom's number. This was the first time she had called her mama from work. Putting her phone on speaker, she pulled open a file she had been working on the day before and hadn't completed yet.

Tess greeted her mama as she did every morning at this time in the language she had been raised in. "Good morning, Mama; it is Tess."

"Terezilya." Her name seemed to bounce off the wall around her.

"Mama, how are you this morning?" She felt a pang of sadness that she wouldn't see her mom for another few months again. It happened every time they talked.

"As good as I can be." It was her mom's usual answer.

"How is Papa?" Tess held her breath. Her mom hadn't said anything about her dad the day before.

"He is Papa. They say his heart is not good anymore, but they don't know him. He is strong as an ox."

"What did they say? The doctors?"

"He needs to take pills, but I don't think he does, Terezilya."

"Mama, he has to take the pills. They went to school, so they know more than you."

"Like you, Terezilya?"

"Do you think I am different from you, Mama?" Tess put down her pen, needing to know what her mother actually thought of her.

"Of course, you are. You have your education and a fancy job,

Terezilya. You have been different since you were a baby," her mama said.

"How was I a different baby?"

"You always had big eyes that saw everything, learned everything. You wouldn't sleep until you were exhausted because you didn't want to miss anything. None of my other babies did that." Her mama rarely talked about her children's childhoods before they came to America.

"Do you like me now?" she asked, needing to know even if she didn't want to hear her answer.

"I love you. You are my baby," her mama said, and Tess could hear the smile in her voice.

"Are you proud of me?" She took her phone off speaker. She didn't need her office walls to hear her mom's disappointment in her.

"Of course, Terezilya. You have done so much in your life, things I could never have dreamed of when you were a baby. Or even when you were a teenager. I couldn't see the future, not the way you could see it." Her mom's voice didn't sound sad like Tess had thought it would.

"But I did not get married and have babies like Ilya and the boys." She admitted.

"But they are not you. You had bigger dreams than that." Her mom said quietly.

"I am going to have a baby, Mama. In six months." Tess held her breath. What would her mother say about an illegitimate grandchild?

"I know, Terezilya, I was just waiting for you to tell me," her mom admitted with a laugh.

Chuckling, Tess asked, "Did Ilya tell you? Tasha?"

"Natasha isn't the only one with the eye. I could see it on you at Easter. Puffy cheeks are the tell." Her mama chuckled at her.

Touching her cheeks, Tess wondered why she couldn't see it. Was it really that noticeable? "Are you mad?"

"That I am going to be a grandmama again? No. Your path has always been different from the others, and this is just another one. I am just happy you will get to be a mama."

"Mama, I have to go, work time." Tess cut the call short as one of the tellers entered the bank.

"Okay," her mama said in English, the only English word either of them had spoken during the conversation, and hung up the phone.

Hanging up with her mama, Tess got up and opened her office door. Melanie walked in and waved good morning to her. Waving back, she went back to her desk. Since winter, she had grown closer to her staff and was now being included more. It seemed that once she made friends outside the bank, she made them inside it.

Tess sat down and picked up her phone, then sent a text to Mathias.

Tess: Are you available tonight?

After hitting send, she knew the day was today. Her mama knew, so now it was time for her baby's dad to find out. She just hoped he would be as understanding as he had been the day before, that he wouldn't be too mad at her for keeping it from him.

She also had to call and decline the job offer. As much as she wanted to work at a larger bank, this was her bank from now on. This was where her family was.

CHAPTER 23

TESS WAS GONE when Math woke up. He had no idea when she had left, but the bed was cold at 5:00 am. *Why didn't she wake him up? Why didn't she say goodbye? How hard would that have been?*

Cora had woken up just as pissed off as he was. So, for the hour it took him to get the kids fed, dressed, and to school, all they did was make each other madder. At least his ex-wife would be picking them up that day. After dropping them off at the school, he wanted to go to the bank and ask Tess why she had left. Seeing that her car wasn't there just made everything worse. After turning on to Main Street, he saw it parked by her front door.

Math parked behind it but didn't know what to do next. Even if her car was at her house, Tess was most likely at the bank—it was only two blocks away. Glancing across the street, he saw his sister Mandy opening the door to her clinic. Math jumped out and crossed the street to talk to her.

"Math, what are you doing in town?" Mandy asked, already behind the reception desk and turning on the computer.

"Dropping off the kids at school."

"So, are you here for personal or professional?"

"Personal. I will not have my big sister seeing me naked." He chuckled at his friend Hue, who always said she had seen the entire town naked—all but Hue, who refused to see her also.

"How personal?" She leaned back in her chair.

"It's about Tess."

"Are congratulations in order?" She held a poker face, giving no indication that she knew anything.

"I guess," he said. He didn't know where their relationship was, but he hoped it was a relationship, even if she left this morning ... or in the middle of the night.

"I am so excited for you two. Her past is amazing, isn't it?" Mandy was smiling bigger than he thought possible.

"Thanks. What she talks about, I guess. But this morning, she left."

Mandy's face dropped instantly. "She took the job?"

"What job?" Scowling at his sister, he demanded.

His sister started to stammer and said, "I, I can't say. I, uh, should not have said anything. But you said...."

"What job, Mandy?" he demanded again.

Her chin went up, and he knew she would never tell him. For his entire life, when she didn't want to, she didn't say anything. It made her a good at keeping secrets and an annoying sister.

Turning, he slammed out of the office and stomped down the street to the bank. *She was leaving? Now? She had to have known she was leaving when she had asked him out. Why did she even do that? Payback for the day on the farm? She said she liked that.*

Once through the door, he saw her sitting behind her desk in her office. Math strode past the receptionist and walked into Tess's office, shutting the door behind him. Maybe slammed it.

"You're leaving?" he asked, glaring down at her.

She looked up at him in confusion. "No?"

"Mandy said you are leaving for a job," he replied, wondering if his sister might just be spreading gossip.

Her gray eyes were big, but her voice remained calm. "Oh, that. I had a job offer, yes. I turned it down."

Not gossip at all, then. It had been true; Tess had been thinking about leaving the entire time. "When?"

She set down her pen and closed the file she was working on. "Today. I called them first thing this morning."

"Why did you ask me out if you were thinking about leaving?" Math crossed his arms over his chest.

The last few days had been amazing, and he wanted nothing more than for this to last forever. He had found the perfect woman, and now she had been thinking about leaving him the entire time. Had it just been a cruel joke on him?

Leaning back in her chair, she looked up at him. He could tell she had her emotions in check today, though she looked like she hadn't slept, which made him wonder exactly when she had left his bed. "Because I wanted to see if we could get along first. Or if you really hated me like you kept saying you did."

"I did not hate you." He knew he had, for a while.

"You wanted me to leave town, Mathias. You said it multiple times. I wanted to see if the real you was the one who wanted me gone or the one who I truly enjoyed spending time with," she stated.

"Why? Why did you even care if you were just going to leave?"

She flinched slightly but recovered quickly, leaving just a stony expression. "Because, Mathias, I am carrying your baby. I wanted to know if you would even want to be a part of her life." Her words hung in the air.

Math went still for a moment before his knees gave out, and he sat heavy in the chair across from her. He couldn't breathe. *Pregnant? No wonder her family was unhappy with her. Was her family so cruel that they would make her miserable from hundreds of miles away?*

"What?" was all he could think to say.

"My birthday."

"We used a condom. I know we did." In his mind, he saw her walking to get it and walking back in nothing but her glorious skin.

"I was on the pill also. Mandy verified it."

"She said congratulations; she thought I already knew. A big congratulations to me." He looked at the ceiling and closed his eyes. Pregnant.

"I can still take the job. I had thought you would be happy. I will just call them and say I can start in a few weeks." She picked up her pen and started to tap it on the desk. "Forget I told you. We will be fine. I do not need you. Just forget it."

His eyes snapped to hers. "I cannot just forget it, Tess. You're carrying my baby."

"We don't know that for sure, Mathias. It is probably someone else's anyway. Just go about your business as usual. You can leave now." He knew she was lying. The baby was his. He didn't get up.

"This job you were thinking about taking... Were you planning on never telling me and just moving away? Taking my child with you?" He could already see Tess holding his baby in her arms.

"If you were the jerk I thought you were, then yes, I was considering it." She started shifting papers on her desk. She didn't look at him.

"The jerk you slept with?" He sneered, because that was what happened that night, just sex.

"Had *sex* with, Mathias," she corrected and picked up her pen.

"Still." Her calmness was getting on his nerves—nerves that were suddenly far more frayed than they had been.

"I am not going to explain myself to you." Her nose flared as she looked up at him.

"How long have you known?" he asked.

"Since Easter. During church."

"So, you sat in front of me and realized you were pregnant with my baby. Then didn't tell me the entire afternoon we spent together?" he demanded.

"No, it was the weekend after that. I was at *my* church, thinking I was going to die of cancer. My periods had stopped, and I talked to my sister, but she said it could not be menopause since I was too young. Then after church, Tasha said I was pregnant," she explained.

"And because your niece said it, it's true?" he questioned, starting to not believe the story.

"Yes." She leaned back in her chair and signed a paper before adding, "No, I took a test the next day, and one with Mandy. But Tasha could already tell."

"When were you going to tell me?" Math folded his arms over his chest. He hated her calmness about this.

"Today."

"Convenient," he hissed.

"It is the truth. That is why I sent you a text to see you tonight." She pointed at her cell phone on her desk.

"I didn't get a text." He pulled out his phone and looked. Nothing. "What happened yesterday?"

"I realized that if I were going to stay here, I would have to give up some things from my past," she stated calmly again. He was starting to realize she worked hard to control her emotions, and most of the time, it worked.

"So, you were depressed because you had to stay here? Sounds like you love it here. Are you going to demand marriage then?" he asked, just like Karen had all those years ago when she got pregnant with Hailey. Would this be another marriage for him that was destined to fail?

"No, we will raise the baby together but separately," she replied.

He glared into her gray eyes. "Why did you sleep with me then?"

"Because I enjoy sex with you," she stated, showing no emotion.

"You're very cold today. It reminds me of the woman I used to know." He shook his head at her and stood up.

"The feeling is mutual," she replied. "Forget I said anything. You are not the person I thought you were."

"Same here, lady. You think I want to have a baby with the cold bitch from the bank?"

They just stared at each other for a while. Her office phone buzzed, and a voice said, "There is someone on line one for you, Tess. If you can't answer, I have no idea who to send them to. I can barely understand them."

Turning away from him, she answered the phone. "Tess Thorn."

Feeling dismissed, Math got up and headed out. He couldn't think straight in her office, surrounded by her smell. She was talking in an even more businesslike tone with the caller as he walked out of her office, slamming the door again. Without a word, he walked out of the bank.

Tess was carrying his baby and had been for months. What was he going to do with her having his baby? Did he even want her to have his baby? She had given him an out; she could leave town, and nobody would ever know. But he would know. He would wonder about the baby. Would it have her gray eyes? Would it have blue? Would the baby look like his family, like his other kids? In the future, would he walk right by his child and never know it was his?

Could he just let her walk away, with or without his baby? He had started his day pissed that she wasn't in bed with him when he woke up. What about when she no longer lived in town? In the state even?

Math stopped and leaned against the brick wall of the bank. He couldn't rap his mind around it. He had gone to the bank because he thought that she was leaving, only to find she was staying and that she was having a baby, their baby.

Math let out a sigh as he pushed away from the wall and headed back into the bank. She would be marrying him. She was having his baby. He walked straight back into her office, but she was gone. The desk was cleared off like she had never been there. Had it all been a dream?

Turning and looking around the bank, he didn't see her. At the reception desk, he asked the middle-aged woman where Tess was.

"She went home sick," the receptionist said, as if she hadn't noticed he had already been in the bank today and had talked to Tess.

"I was standing outside the door, and I didn't see her."

"She probably went out the back door. It's a shorter walk to her apartment that way." She pointed toward the back of the building, but Math didn't see a door in that direction.

The moment she said, 'back door,' he knew she was gone. Rushing out the door, he headed to her apartment. Had she accepted the other job? Was she already leaving? He was practically running when he made it down the street and bounded up the stairway.

He pounded on the door once and tried to walk in. But the door was locked; it didn't budge. Pounding on it again, he yelled her name, but she didn't answer. Swearing, he turned and went down the stairs into the morning sun. That's when he saw her car was gone. Where the old red Chevrolet sat was an empty parking spot.

Now what? He thought. He couldn't scour the countryside, looking for her. And what would he do when he found her? Chase her car around?

Math pulled out his phone to call Hue to see if he had seen her if he was on patrol. Instead, he saw he had a text from her. Not only had the one she said she sent earlier come through but also one that said:

Tess: She is mine. Forget I said anything.

As if that was going to be possible. The woman he was starting to fall in love with was carrying his baby. And he had messed up so bad that she was gone.

After checking with everyone in her book club that he knew, he climbed the steps and sat in front of her door. She would eventually come back and need to get into her house. He would be there when that happened.

CHAPTER 24

A FIGHT *with Mathias will not interfere with my job,* she decided as she picked up the phone even as he was yelling at her.

Turning her back on Mathias, she answered the phone, "Tess Thorn, President."

"Terezilya, it's Ilya," her sister said in Russian.

"What are you calling me at work for?" Tess was a bit angry at her sister. She turned just in time to see Mathias leaving her office.

"It's Papa. I couldn't get you to answer the other phone," Ilya replied just as angrily.

"What about Papa?" Tess said, turning on her cell phone.

"Mama called the ambulance a few minutes ago. I don't know much, but I think you have to come. Now." Her sister sounded panicked.

"I will." She hung up her phone and watched her cell phone show missed calls from Ilya, Tasha, and her brother, Mike.

Pain and anger at Mathias turned to worry and fright for her father in an instant. Clearing her desk, she put the files away and went down to Logan Tucker's office; he was the vice president. After knocking on his door, she explained that she had a family emergency and was heading home. He was understanding and said for her to go and call when she knew anything.

Hurrying out of the bank, she went straight to her car. No need to pack; she could borrow everything she needed from her family when she got home.

Home. Would she make it in time to see her father one last time, or was she going to miss that? If she had just married and stayed there, she would have been there with him. Why had she always been so selfish?

Straight from the bank, she climbed into her sanctuary, the one place she was herself in the middle of a foreign land. Her car was her refuge now. It was the only thing that could take her home and the only place she felt at home. Familiar.

Tess called Ilya as she headed out of town to see if there was an update on her father's condition. She hoped she hadn't already lost her father.

"Terezilya, you are speaking in English again!" Ilya scolded her.

"Ilya, it is just as easy for you to translate it as it is for me to."

"No, it is not. You know I don't know all the words you do. And you hate when I ask what something means."

"I do not."

"You do. That's why you need to speak Russian."

"I am not going to keep speaking Russian just for you."

"You can't stop speaking the language of your birth, Terezilya."

"You have no idea what I can and cannot do."

Ilya huffed. After a moment, she asked, "Are you bringing home your man?"

"No, he does not belong there," Tess stated firmly. Whatever had happened between them these last few days, it was over now. He hated her again. This time with good reason.

"You cannot hide who you are."

"I can and I will," she argued.

"Forever?"

"Yes, if that's how long it takes."

"What about when you come home?"

"My trips there will stop when Mama and Papa are gone." She hadn't meant to tell her. She was just planning to let it happen. Nobody would notice then.

"This is your home, Terezilya. Forever!" Ilya yelled at her, something her sister rarely did.

"No, Ilya, it has not been my home for a long time," Tess reminded her sister, though her sister had never once seen any of the places she lived over the years.

"This is your home," Ilya stated firmly.

"*This* is my home, Ilya, and this is where my child will be raised. That means that I need to be here. We will have to be American. I have to stop being Russian for her, Ilya."

"You can stop being Russian, Terezilya, but you will forever be a part of this family," Ilya replied, calmer now than she had been before.

"You do not know, Ilya, because you have never left. I have been apart from you guys for almost twenty years. I have to just walk away because I don't fit in anyway." Tess felt a tear run down her cheek. Her anger had subsided, and now she was just left with pain.

"You have chosen to keep everything in little boxes, but all those boxes make you Tess. Even the ones that say Terezilya on them," Ilya said quietly.

"I have to go. I will call you when I am closer," Tess replied, ending the call. She didn't know if Ilya would call back, but she assumed Ilya would call Tasha first.

Looking around, she realized that she was a few miles past the turn-off to Mathias's house. But she had no time to stop, no time to just let him hold her until some of the pain of losing her father forever was gone.

Without any warning, her little car shuddered and sputtered for a moment, then shut off completely despite the speed she was going. Steering became nearly impossible, making Tess hit the ditch at a speed that propelled her through a clump of trees. The front of her car hit one large enough to stop her instantly—it was only the airbag that prevented her head from slamming into the steering wheel.

Sitting silently in the middle of a tree grove in her now destroyed little red car, her sanctuary, her only way home, Tess tried to start the engine again. Maybe? But nothing happened. It turned over, but no sound came, and no engine roared to life. Her little car was dead, and with it, her way home and the last little bit of who she was.

CHAPTER 25

Taking out his phone, he looked at her text again. How could he respond to that? What could he say to make her see he had messed up? Maybe he should just call and see if she would answer. But he knew better than that; she wouldn't answer him regardless.

"Hey, Hue," he said as the phone in his hand rang.

"Morning, Math." Hue's formal tone made Math stop. Something was up.

"What's wrong?"

"I'm about a mile north of your place. Tess is okay." Hue's words made Math's blood run cold. Why would he say she was okay? Was it possible she wouldn't be okay? "But her car is not. She went off the road and hit a tree."

"Is she hurt?" Math asked in concern, getting up from the floor and heading down the steps.

"Yes, it wasn't bad. But she won't get out of the car."

"You've talked to her?" Pushing through the door into the warm sun, he quickly went to his truck still in the bank parking lot.

"Yep. She says if you give it a minute, it will start again. It won't. Norm won't get to it until late tonight, maybe tomorrow," Hue said.

"I'll be there in a minute." Math climbed into his pickup and headed toward his place.

Minutes later, he pulled up behind Hue's cruiser, stopping to talk to his friend who was leaning against his car. "She's still in there. Says the tow truck is on its way. I really don't think Norm is coming out today. Estelle kicked him out again last night, and he went on his usual bender. Still in lockup as far as I know."

Math ignored the gossip and asked again, "But she is fine?"

"She was going at a good speed when she hit the ditch. The ditch slowed her down, but the airbag deployed when she hit the tree. I think something happened with the car to cause it to go off the road," Hue surmised.

"She really likes that car." Math looked at the red car with the crumpled front end resting against a small tree. He then saw her in the front seat with her head resting on the steering wheel.

"I will leave you to her. Call if you need me." Hue said as Math walked down the ditch toward her.

Walking around to the passenger side of the car, he opened the door and slid inside next to her. Her head was still on the steering wheel, and she didn't acknowledge that he was there. Though she was not crying, it really seemed she was beyond tears, like her life was as ruined as the little old car she sat in.

"Tess, are you okay?" he asked, reaching out and touching her blonde hair.

"I.... The tow truck is coming." She seemed confused.

"But are you okay?" He asked again.

"Yes."

"Can we go home?" he asked.

"I cannot go home again," she whispered into the steering wheel.

"You can always go home. Nobody is ever going to stop you." He wanted to touch her, but he didn't know how she would react to that.

"I think my car is broken." The hood was so smashed up you couldn't see out of the windshield. The car was never going anywhere again.

"We will get you another one."

"But this is my car. I bought this one," she insisted.

"You can buy another. An even nicer one." He reached over and rubbed her back. When she didn't pull away, he kept doing it.

"But another one will not be this one, and I need this one." She didn't move, didn't look at him.

"Tess, you will have to get a new car for the baby anyway. This will just make it happen a little quicker"

"For the baby. I have to give up everything for the baby. You are right." Her voice was as calm and collected as when she had told him he couldn't have the loan. Just as cold and unfeeling.

"Tess, it isn't like that. You don't have to give up *everything* for the baby." Having no idea what she was talking about, he wondered if she was in shock from the accident.

"But I do, Mathias. I just thought I would have this a little longer. I thought…"

"What is so special about this car?" He wanted to know.

"I bought it new. It was supposed to last forever." She sighed, head still on the steering wheel.

He smiled. "Cars don't last forever."

"This one had to. I told my papa it would." Her voice cracked a little at the words.

"I think he will understand when it doesn't."

"I will never know. He is dying today. I cannot get there, and my car is broken." Tears were coming out of her eyes, but she showed no emotion as she said the words.

"We'll take my pickup," he said, getting out of the car. When she didn't follow, he went to her door and pulled her out. She grabbed her phone, and he grabbed her briefcase and purse from the back seat.

"No, it is a sign. I will not go," she stated firmly, trying to grab her bags from him.

Math just gently pushed her toward his truck. "So, without this car, you cannot go home? Ever? No other car can drive there?"

After loading her into his pickup, he drove back to his place. When he parked, she did not get out of the pickup; she just stared out the passenger window at the farm. But he didn't think she really saw anything.

Math hurried into the house and packed a bag for himself. When he got back to the pickup, she was still there. Her phone was ringing when he got into the cab, but she wasn't moving to pick it up. For a moment, he wondered if she was actually hurt from the accident, but it didn't matter—they had a nine-hour drive in front of them. No way was she not going to be there if her dad was dying today.

They had been on the road for over an hour before her phone had stopped ringing, but she had yet to look at her messages. He hadn't said anything to her; it was up to her to talk. Knowing how he would feel if his dad were sick and he was far away from him, he let her just do what she wanted to do.

"You do not have to take me, Mathias. I chose not to be there a long time ago." She didn't turn away from the passenger window.

He wondered if she really thought he would just turn around and drive her back to Landstad. Did she realize how many miles they had already traveled? Did she realize how much he would do for her just because she asked? Or in this case, didn't ask?

"You have put a lot on a car, Tess. It's just a car."

Her head came up, but she leaned it back against the seat and closed her eyes. "When I went to college, Alex, Tasha, and I went looking for a car for me. I needed to get to Fargo and back, and though I was living on campus, I would need a job. A full-ride scholarship does not mean everything's paid for. So, we found this nice old car. It was big and older than I was, but it ran, and the three of us felt it would be a good one for me to have. I brought it home, and Papa hated it, said it would never last more than a few miles. He said that I would have to walk home, and I would be done with the college thing. He was against my leaving in the first place, I knew that, but it still hurt to hear the words."

Rubbing her hands over her face, she continued, "The car made it to Fargo. And it made it another week. But then it was done. He was right, of course, about the car. But there was no way I was leaving college—that had been my dream. No car meant I had no way home.

For four years, I went home only during the summer for a few weeks. I took the bus then. In the dorm rooms, I would watch parents come and get their kids and bring them home for Thanksgiving, Christmas, Easter. Not mine."

"Did you ask?" He took her hand in his.

"Yes, once. The first Christmas, I asked my mom if Papa could come and get me. Papa said no, I had made my decision. I left."

"He doesn't feel that way anymore," he tried to assure her.

"When I bought this car, I had just gotten a divorce. They did not approve or attend the wedding. I had a good job and needed a way to get to work that was not the bus. I found this car, and it was so cute, and I loved it. The next time I went home, I was excited to show off my first new car. I had made it. Papa barely looked at it and said it would never last a year, just like my first car. He said when it died, I would be walking again, and he was not going to come and get me. But my car did not die that first year or ever within the last ten. She has always been there for me. She has never let me down. She lets me be me, no matter what."

"She is just a car, Tess. You can drive any car, and it will take you back there. Your dad's opinion ten years ago shouldn't change that."

"He is right; I made my decision. Since I drove away in that old car, I knew that every time I went back, I was just putting off the inevitable. That one day, I would have to stop. I would just have to be an American," Tess said. "Now I will do that; the past is over. For the baby, I will look forward."

He had no idea how to argue with her. She was not making any sense. They sat in silence, and he realized that she had cried herself to sleep, silent tears that she had been unable to control.

Picking up his phone, he called his sister. When she answered, he rushed to explain, "Mandy, Tess was in a car accident. She is making no sense. I don't know what to do."

"Is she okay?" Mandy sounded concerned, but she was a nurse and knew that Tess was pregnant.

"Physically, yes, but her dad is sick. I'm driving her home," he said, hoping he wasn't making a mistake by not making her see a doctor before they left.

"How is she acting?" Mandy asked.

"Like talking that she can't go home again, like that she and the baby have to be Americans, whatever that means," he said, knowing he sounded just as odd as Tess had.

"Math, Math, Math, I can't say anything. But please, please ask her about her childhood. Over the years, she has built a wall around her past. You need to get through that wall. I think she has been making it higher since she found out she was pregnant. But her past is so much of her that the wall is crushing her." Mandy's words were like a riddle, one he didn't know if he had the strength to solve that day.

"I really am tired of people giving me cryptic replies," Math said to his sister, but his eyes were on Tess just sitting in the pickup, lost in her own world alone in the vehicle.

"Just trust me. If you think you love her now, wait until you meet the real her."

"I am not in love with her, Mandy." As he hung up on her, he knew he was lying. But he didn't need his sister to tell him he didn't know the real woman he was in love with. The call had made everything worse. As the hours slipped by, he watched her sleep. She was mumbling more than usual. Some people snored, but Tess was a talker. Not loud and not with actual words, but she talked faster in her mumbling.

At just after hour five, his phone rang. It was Tasha, so he answered it.

"Is Tessy with you? We cannot get a hold of her," the woman said.

"Yes," he replied and heard her tell others that Tess had been found.

"Ilya said she wasn't bringing you," Tasha stated.

"She hit a tree with her car. How is your dad? I mean, grandpa?" he asked.

"So far, okay. I don't know much, big words," Tasha stated as if that was an excuse to not know what was going on. "How far are you?"

"GPS has four hours left," Math stated.

"Good, you will be here close to six." He heard her tell others the time they would get in. "Can I talk to her?" Tasha asked with hope in her voice.

"She's asleep. I'll try and get her to call when she wakes up."

"Tell her to call her mama." Tasha hung up on him.

"Tasha?" he heard from across the car. Tess's gray eyes were on him.

Nodding in answer, he asked, "Are you feeling better?"

"No," was all she said. "But nothing with the baby, just my emotions."

"You need to call your … mama." Tripping over the word, he wondered if their baby would call her Mama or Mom. He hoped it would be the former. Knowing that if he got a say, it would be, Tess was a Mama. "I mean, your mom. You say 'mama' better than I do."

"I will call her." But she made no move to actually do that, just sat with her head resting on the seat's back.

"Why didn't you want me to come with you? When you went off the road, you weren't going to my place. You were leaving town." He looked over at her, but she was just looking out the windshield at the cars in front of them.

"I am keeping my past and present separate." She shrugged as she adjusted in the seat.

"How are you planning on doing that?"

"Easy. I will stop going there, and I will stop talking to them. They do not leave. The baby cannot live in two worlds. I am picking one. Yours." She leaned her head back and shut her eyes.

"Because of me?" Though he knew the answer, he wanted her to say it.

"The baby belongs in your world."

"Do you belong in my world?" he asked, not knowing how their worlds could be that different. They had a lot in common, after all.

"I have been in neither world for so long, I do not know where I belong."

"With me?"

"I thought so, but after you see my family, you will not want me anymore." Opening her eyes, she turned to him. She had said it so matter of fact.

"Do you think that bad of me?" Math knew he hadn't been on his best behavior around her most of the time, but he didn't think seeing her family would change his feelings for her.

"Not you in particular. My husband left me after he met my family. He wanted someone I couldn't be."

"Just because you married an ass doesn't mean all men are asses," he said and then added, "Even if I was in the beginning, I hope you know I have changed."

"We will see." She said but didn't crack a smile at his joke.

Since she was awake, they stopped for gas and food and were off again. All the while, she had complained that it was not the gas station she always stopped at. As they were headed out, she took off the blazer she had been wearing for hours.

Tess kicked her shoes off and pulled the bun out of her hair, and Math thought she looked more relaxed than he had seen since the day before in her shower. Since they hadn't talked about it, he wondered if it was because of her dad being sick or because of the baby. Either way, he knew he hadn't helped her. In fact, he had hindered her far more—something he wasn't going to let happen again.

Once back on the road, she started to go through her texts and calls. There must have been a lot because it took almost half an hour to get through them. Some she answered, some she didn't. All the while, she had been eating pretzels. When she rolled up the bag, she said, "I have to call my mama."

"Go ahead," he replied. It wasn't like he was going to stop so that she could talk in private. If she wanted that, she should have said something at the gas station.

"She is Russian." She was watching him closely as she tucked her foot under her leg.

"I know, you said you were Russian once," he said, looking at the road. But his mind was on her tattoo. He had yet to spend enough time looking at it.

"I will be speaking to her in Russian. She understands English, but she does not speak it. I do not want her to have to translate today."

"You can speak Russian?" He turned and looked at her. He couldn't imagine her speaking a foreign language.

"Yes."

"How well? I mean, I can speak a little Spanish." Though he had taken a class in high school, there was no way he could have any type of conversation in it now.

"My mother does not speak English. Do you speak the language your mother speaks?" she questioned him with a raised eyebrow.

"Yes, I do, smarty pants. Make your call." He reached over and pushed a strand of hair behind her ear.

Turning back to the road, he let her see that he would not eavesdrop on her call. But it only took a word or two for him to realize he would have no idea what she was saying anyway. Not only was she speaking another language, but she was speaking with a speed he had never heard before.

As she continued to talk to her mom, the realization hit him hard: she spoke Russian in her sleep. It was not mumbling at all. It was her speaking in another language. And it was the language she spoke when they'd had sex.

Math looked at her, but she turned away from him, continuing her conversation. She was blushing, and he wondered if they were both thinking about when they made love. Her reaction said yes.

Abruptly, she switched to English, said another word in Russian, and the next in English. "Doctor Jones, this is Tess Thorn. Alex Aleksandrov is my father."

Math couldn't hear what the doctor said, but her response was, "I speak English, so you can tell me what is happening."

Then she listened and asked questions with ease. Reaching into her briefcase, she pulled out a pen and paper and started to write down notes. Then she would refer back to the notes with questions. From her side of the conversation, Math had gathered that her father had a heart attack and would be having surgery in the morning.

The phone on the other end must have been given back to her

family because she was suddenly back to speaking Russian, and based on her tapping and underlining words, she was explaining what the doctor had told her. It seemed like they relied on her knowledge of the language to tell them what was going on. But why wouldn't her siblings know enough English? Her nieces and nephews? Why was it up to her?

Was this the two worlds she was talking about? One where she was a bank president and one where her parents didn't even speak English? But hadn't she been living between the two worlds for years? Why would a baby change that?

Math had no idea what the answer was, and he wasn't going to ask Tess until they were sure her father was going to be all right. He was here for her, not to be another burden she had to manage.

CHAPTER 26

TRYING NOT to look at Mathias, Tess tried to explain what the doctor had told her to her family. She could tell that the man was happy to speak to someone who spoke English. Though his attitude grated on her nerves, she had controlled her anger. It wouldn't help anyone to blow up at the man. Her mom was far more relaxed after her daughter had told her what was actually happening. If her father did well during the surgery, he would be better for a while. He would live.

"How far away are you?" her mom asked anxiously.

"I am almost there," Tess said, trying to hold back her tears.

"Then we will talk," her mama replied ominously. She must have been told.

"No, Mama, this is not the time to talk. We can talk another time," Tess said quietly. She would have to tell her mother that she was staying in Landstad with the baby, that she would never be any closer than that for the rest of her mom's life.

"Ilya is here." She knew with the words that her mom was handing off the phone.

"Terezilya, where are you?" her sister asked.

Tess repeated what she had said to her mom. And added that they weren't planning any more stops between here and there.

"Are you driving?" Ilya demanded.

"No, Mathias is driving," she assured her sister as she looked over at the man. His eyes were on the road, but she knew he had figured out that she spoke Russian in bed. It hadn't taken him very long to figure it out.

"Good, you can't drive when you are emotional. Are you staying with me?"

"No, you have your kids home. We will get a hotel," Tess said the dreaded H word to her sister.

"You cannot stay at a hotel! They cost money, Terezilya. I will make room. No, Natasha, do you have room for Terezilya and her man?" Tess listened to her sister asking her niece. She didn't think that Tasha would make room for two. It had always been manageable to squeeze one more in their full house, but two was going to be impossible.

"I will get a hotel. It is fine. I will make him pay," she lied and didn't say Mathias's name—he might notice if she said his name.

"No, No, Tasha said her house. She will make room," Ilya said. Tess didn't know if Tasha agreed to it or not. Ilya was a force when she wanted to be.

"It is already paid for, Ilya. Mathias is not used to all the people. He will need to get away." She stole another glance over at the man, who she couldn't imagine sleeping on Tasha's couch. And if he got the couch, where would she sleep?

"How is the baby?" Ilya asked. She must have decided Tess was right.

"She is good, no worries," Tess replied. The baby was the last thing on her mind at the moment. "You come to the hospital, then go to Tasha's. I will see you when I get there."

As Tess hung up, she leaned her head against the back of her seat and shut her eyes. Now she needed to make a hotel reservation.

"How was everyone? You talked to more than one person, right? And a doctor?" Mathias asked from beside her. Had he been paying attention to her call? How could he have known she spoke with two people?

"Yes, I spoke with Mama and Ilya. How did you know?" She looked over at him.

"Because after a while, you started to speak a mixture of Russian and English. We are getting a hotel, so you don't have to stay with your niece." He smiled at her lie.

She stared at him in shock. She did not speak English. "No, I do not think I did."

"Speak English and Russian interchangeably? Yes, you switched over every few words. But you talk a lot faster in Russian."

"It is the language I was raised on," she finally admitted. "I do not have to think as much when I speak it."

"You have to think about English?" he asked.

"I did not learn English until I was six, so yes." She hated telling people that.

"When you went to school?"

She shook her head. She had to tell him; after all, he would know all too soon. "No, when I left Russia. I did not go to school until I was closer to eight."

"You're pulling my leg, Tess. You have no accent. Your niece has an accent," Math said.

Chuckling, she said, "And Tasha was born in Wisconsin."

"Why did you come at six?"

"Eight. We came to the US when I was eight. We spent eighteen months in England, waiting to come over. I first learned British English. I was the only one who could speak it when we came over," she told him, watching his face for any sign he thought she wasn't like other girls.

"And now? Do they speak it now?"

"Most do, but Mama does not, and Papa does not want to."

"You talk in your sleep all the time. I thought you were just mumbling, but you were speaking in Russian." He tucked a curl behind her ear, and his hand lingered as it skated across her jaw.

"I do not talk in my sleep." Nobody had ever told her that before.

"Not going to argue the Russian part?" His hand caught hers and held it.

Still holding his hand, she turned away and mumbled, "My dreams are in Russian. Almost always."

"You once said you were in speech therapy. Was it for your accent? I assume you used to have one." He squeezed her hand, not letting it go as he drove.

Tess turned back to him, surprised he remembered she'd said that. "Yes, it was horrid. The school I chose had a great speech therapist who helped me a great deal. Then I worked on it at college."

"Is that why you don't use contractions?"

"What are you talking about?" Suddenly, she realized he might be more attuned to her than she had thought.

"At Easter, Kit said you don't use contractions, and you don't. Ever." He shifted but held fast to her hand.

"My speech therapist suggested I not use them. By not using them, it slows down my speech so that I can concentrate on the big words while I say more little words," she explained, shutting her eyes.

"So, you dream in Russian. What about that little voice in your head?"

"I must translate every word I say so that you know what I am saying." She admitted her secret. But when he met her family, he would know every little thing about her.

"Mandy was right. You are amazing."

"Mandy was not supposed to tell you." She shook her head at her friend. Maybe she wasn't so different from her loose-lipped cousin as she liked to think.

"She only said that you were amazing—nothing else. You really came to this country at six?" he asked again as if he couldn't believe it.

"Eight, when I met Tasha. And I met my four brothers who had already been here for years, and some I had never met before. They were mostly already married with kids. Tasha is married to Alex, who is my nephew, but Tasha is my other brother's stepdaughter, so they are cousins. They have eight children, and Ilya has eighteen with a few stepchildren. You were nervous because you didn't think I would get along with your children. I have been around children all my life."

"No wonder the noise and confusion on Easter didn't faze you."

"Your family is very small," she told him. Easter was nothing compared to what he was walking into tonight. He didn't know what noise and confusion really was. Tomorrow he would. She just hoped he was still around tomorrow.

CHAPTER 27

THE GPS HAD him turning toward a small hospital. In the parking lot, they found a space and quickly went into the building. At the front desk, Tess was back to all business. "What room is Alex Aleksandrov in?"

The lady behind the desk looked up at her quizzically, reminding Math of people back home who knew a name and had to put that face to a name. "The room is down the hallway to the left. Do you want me to take you?" The woman spoke very slowly and a bit louder than was needed.

"No, we will find it," Tess said dismissively.

Following her down the hallway, he couldn't really believe a receptionist had spoken down to her. The woman had her own receptionist! But these people knew her family as an immigrant family, less than a local. Which made him realize why his words that winter about her not being from around here had hurt her. She had heard them all before.

"I will probably speak to everyone in Russian. I cannot guarantee that I will translate things for you. Not today. I want to stop worrying about my father before I can worry about you. If you want to go to a hotel now, that is fine," she suggested, offering him an out on meeting her family, a way for him to walk away.

Taking her hand, he made her stop and turn to him. "I am here for you. Don't worry about me, ever."

She gave him a weak smile. "This might not be easy."

"Nothing has been with you so far. Why would today be any different?" He pulled her into his arms and kissed her.

As he pulled his lips from hers, he looked into her worried eyes. He wanted to stop that worry. A loud yell from down the hallway made her tense. Then she breathed, "Mikhail."

Pushing out from his arms, she turned to her brother—the oldest one, he assumed. Math looked at the man standing at the end of the hallway and was taken aback by her brother. He had expected a large man with a large attitude, but the man in front of them was older, skinny, and short. Tess gave him a hug, and Math saw that Tess was taller than her brother by a few inches, and her heels made her even taller.

"Mikhail, this is Mathias Nordskov. Mathias, my brother, Mike."

Math shook his hand. The man's grip indicated he was more powerful than he looked. This was a man who had worked hard his entire life. In a heavy accent, the man said, "Go in and see Papa. I will stay out here with your man."

Without a word, Tess turned and walked into the room behind them. Mike let go of his hand and looked him up and down. His voice was not angry or happy when he asked, "Are you the father then?"

"You were told?" Apparently, word gets out fast in this family.

"No, she has the look. You can't hide it," he said with a laugh. "Terezilya has always tried not to be an Aleksandrov, but deep down, she is."

It took a moment for Math to realize who Terezilya was. Mike was referring to Tess. He wondered why she didn't use her real name, it was beautiful.

"She goes by Tess." Mathias felt the need to point out.

"And I go by Mike, but my family still calls me Mikhail. She is Tess Thorn, bank president. She is the only one of us kids who went to high school." The man didn't mention her graduating from private school or with a four-year degree from a university.

"She says that your family is not proud of her." Math crossed his arms.

"She's different, always was. The first day I saw her, she was eight, I suppose. She was in pants, and none of the other women in our family wore pants then, just dresses and skirts. But she wore pants, so she was different. Now everyone wears pants." He was smiling at the memory.

"Why didn't anyone go get her when she was in college and couldn't get home?" Math pushed. He had no reason for this man to like him, and Tess needed answers about her past to get beyond it.

"Nobody had money or a car that would go that far back then. In those days, each family really only had one car, and everyone had little kids. Today, nobody has money for a trip, and she is even farther away."

Math felt like that was a thin excuse. "Why does everyone have a cell phone then? How do you have enough money for those?"

"Terezilya pays the phone bills, always has. That's why the women have the phones." He looked at him, but Math could tell it embarrassed him to admit it.

"What else does she pay for?" Math knew there was more that she took care of. He saw her apartment, and she wasn't saving that money.

"Most of my parents' upkeep. If anyone falls on hard times, Terezilya is called," Mike admitted. Math could tell the old man resented his sister for her ability to help those who needed it.

Tess's demeanor was better when she walked out of the hospital room. Ignoring her brother, she turned to Math and said, "Papa wants to meet you in case he dies."

Math couldn't tell if she was making a joke or if that was what the man was really saying. She took his hand and led him into the hospital room, willing to show him some affection in front of her family.

You would have never convinced him these were her parents on the day he had applied for a loan. Not in a million years. He knew they were eighty or close to it, but they both looked old beyond their years. Her father was an older version of her brother: small, frail, and tired-looking. The woman who wrapped him into a tight hug was exactly what he'd expected: a little old lady with gray hair and Tess's eyes. She was talking to him, but she was talking in Russian, so he couldn't understand.

"Mama says she is happy to meet you, happy she lived long enough to see you," Tess said, rolling her eyes at the last bit. He knew she was translating word for word, not changing it to save herself from embarrassment.

"Nice to meet you," he replied. Tess didn't translate what he said.

But before he could question her, the woman was talking again. But this time, Tess was arguing with her. Math just watched. Tess was speaking so fast and waving at the woman and sometimes at him with her hands, something he had rarely seen her do when she spoke English.

"Mama says that Tasha has a bed for us. She will not let us stay at a hotel," Tess said, looking down at her mom with a frown on her face. Her mom had a huge smile as she looked at him. Tess had lost the argument, it seemed.

"Listen to your mama, Terezilya," her father said in English from the bed. "Mathias Nordskov. Sounds Russian."

"Sorry, sir, it's Danish." Math could see how much the older couple adored their daughter.

The old man only nodded as he said, "I am going to say Russian."

"Papa, you cannot just tell people they are Russian. He is not." Tess slipped her hand in his as she said the words.

"I am dying. Let me die knowing he is Russian. Now it is late, and you had a long drive, Terezilya. You go to Natasha and Alex's house now. Rest." Her father dismissed her.

Glancing at his watch, he realized it was after 9:00 pm, and it had been a long day. Though Tess had slept some during the drive, she looked exhausted now that she had been able to see her father. He let her hand go so that she could hug her parents, then led her out of the hospital room. Mike was still in the hallway, and Math assumed the man would stay there until morning in case his parents needed him. Tess gave Mike a hug, and they headed out of the hospital.

At the truck, he told her to drive since she knew how to get to her niece's house. Though he half expected her to go to a hotel instead, he was happy when she headed out of town.

"Tasha has sent the boys to my parents for the night, so we will have a bed. But it is still going to be busy. And morning will come early," she warned.

"It's okay, Tess. This is where you usually stay, isn't it?"

"Yes, but I only get the couch. Tasha is giving you a bedroom," she told him.

"She doesn't want to scare me off. Did your ex get a room, or was he with you on the couch?" He put his hand on her shoulder.

"Neither. He went to a hotel. He insisted that he couldn't sleep in a house with so many people or spend a lot of time with people who would not just speak English. He never came back, and we were divorced within months." Her grip on the steering wheel was tight.

"He was a moron."

"Thanks. But again, I cannot make sure everyone speaks English, and I cannot translate everything all the time."

"Except for your parents, shouldn't they all know English?"

"Just Mama does not; she understands it, though. She just chooses not to speak it. The rest of the family should, so just call them out on it," she said, more to the road than to him.

So, her mom didn't need the translating that he needed. She understood everything he had said. And he had a suspicion that she might know more English than she let on. Having Tess talk for her was maybe her way of having her daughter know how important she was.

"Okay, so I will just demand they speak to me," he joked.

"Sorry, you are right. I will talk to them." Her eyes went back to the road.

"I was kidding. Mike was nice to me, and I assume the rest will be the same. He asked if I was the baby's dad," he told her in case she didn't know how many people already knew.

Her eyes turned to him. "What? They will all know by tomorrow."

"Does he have *the eye*?" he questioned her with a laugh.

"Not really, but most in the family can tell. Even I can usually tell, just not apparently about me." She admitted.

Looking at her in the glow of the dash lights, he couldn't see that she looked any different then she had before. Though she acted differently with her family, more relaxed.

Pulling into a long driveway, he saw a house in front of him that had almost every light on. As she parked in front of it, the door flew open, and two women came out, hugged Tess, and pulled her into the house. Math grabbed his lone bag from the back seat and headed toward the house alone.

As he approached the door, it opened for him, and a man let him into the house. Seeing the man in the light, he was surprised that he looked so much like Tess. Math would have pegged the guy as a brother, but he knew this was her nephew.

"This way, Mathias. I am Alex; Tessy is my aunt." The man smiled and led him to a small bedroom upstairs that contained two sets of bunk beds, all with matching homemade quilts. The room was too small for all the furniture and stuff in it, but it looked comfortable.

"Thank you, Alex," Math said, putting the suitcases on the bed.

"Anytime. We love having Tessy back. She is missed when she is gone," he stated and led him back downstairs. "The girls are talking. They will talk for a long time."

Math saw them in the kitchen around the table. They were speaking in Russian and were mostly laughing. He knew that they had just picked up in the middle of a conversation that had been started on the phone at some point. It was something he was getting used to.

When he walked into the room, the women immediately switched to English but continued to talk about Tess's parents for a few moments.

"Mathias, this is Tasha and Ilya." Tess pointed at the two women. Tasha was nothing like he thought. She was dark to Tess's light. Dark brown eyes and almost black hair, she was short and round. But her smile was as large as her niece's at being together again.

Ilya, on the other hand, was Tess in a few years. She was a mirror into her future. Her hair was still blonde, and her gray eyes were on him. There was no big smile for Ilya, however. She was suspicious of him.

"Hello, Mathias. Thank you for bringing Terezilya to us," Ilya stated in a heavy accent.

"I am glad she let me," he admitted, knowing how close she was to traveling there by herself.

"I am surprised she let you as well. Terezilya is stubborn," Ilya said.

"Like grandpa," Alex chimed in from the doorway.

"No, no," Tasha said with a laugh. "Tessy is way more stubborn than grandpa."

"Hey, I am right here." Tess rolled her eyes.

"Imagine what we say when you are not," Ilya joked at her little sister.

"I know what you say when I am not here," she said to Ilya, then turned to Math, "She sometimes forgets I am on the group texts."

"I-I cannot keep it all straight," Ilya stammered out her excuse and then laughed heartily. "I sound like Mama."

"You always sound like Mama." Tasha laughed.

"Are you two hungry? Tasha has food," Ilya stated, jumping up as if she just remembered they hadn't been fed yet.

"See? Mama." Tess laughed at her sister.

"I will force-feed you if I have to, Terezilya. Remember how she used to say that to you? Then you would have to sit at the table for hours until everything on your plate was gone," Ilya said, taking things out of the fridge.

"All the time," Tess replied quietly.

"Does she eat yet, Mathias? She is so picky," Ilya asked him.

"I don't notice that she is picky, but she doesn't eat much," he said. He was still concerned about it, even after his talk with Mandy. After all, she was eating for two now.

"Eat, Terezilya," Ilya said to her sister and put a plate in front of her.

Tess looked at the plate and pushed it away. "I will not eat that. I know exactly what it is."

"Picky, Picky." Ilya took the plate back with a cackle, putting it back in the fridge.

Math had no idea what was on the plate, but he was glad he hadn't been offered whatever it was. No way would he have eaten it either.

"Come on, Mathias, let the ladies talk. They will be here for hours." Alex showed him to the living room.

Alex sat in an old armchair, and Math sat on the couch that didn't match at all but was well worn. From his spot, he could see the women and hear them, but they had slipped back into a hybrid of Russian and English.

"She is happy. She isn't always," Alex stated, pulling Math's attention to the man.

"You've known her all her life?" Math asked.

"Since she was eight, and I was ten. I knew then that she didn't belong. She was different." His eyes were trained on the kitchen also.

Math was still looking at him. "That's how Mike says it also, different."

"She is. You will see tomorrow."

"She thinks your family is keeping things about her parents from her."

"I don't know. I think everyone is having trouble with them getting old. I mean, they have always been old, but they will die soon. Ilya's first husband is the only person to have died in the family since leaving Russia. There are no aunts and uncles or grandparents, so they don't know what to do with death. They are all scared about it," Alex said.

"I understand, but it's hurting her feelings." Math watched her talking with her family with a smile he rarely saw back in Landstad.

Alex's eyes followed Math's to the women. "They will talk all night, especially after Tessy hasn't been texting as much as normal."

"Why not?" His eyes went back to her nephew.

"Tessy's having a hard time with the baby." Alex ran a hand over his hair.

"She hasn't said that." Math looked at her, who was now pointing at her sister and laughing.

He wished for the moments back when she'd told him about the baby. This time he would be excited and tell her that they should raise it together. He wanted to be with her forever.

Alex shook his head. "She won't. She is stubborn like grandma."

Math chuckled. "You mean like your grandpa?"

"No, grandma is the more stubborn one. She could have learned to speak English over the years, but she didn't want her family to forget where they came from, so she didn't. Tess would do that in a heartbeat."

"Is that a warning?" Math asked, grinning.

"Nope, just something for you to know. But I have to get up early, so I am going to bed." Alex got up and ventured into the kitchen, only to get teased for kissing his wife goodnight and for going to bed so early.

Following Alex's lead, Math walked into the kitchen and kissed Tess on the head, telling her that he was going to bed as well. The drive had been too much, and he was exhausted. Tess said she would come up when she got tired, and the other women said nothing in English. In Russian, they exchanged comments as he walked out of the room with a smile, knowing that Tess was going to be teased more than he was.

CHAPTER 28

It was close to 3:00 am when she crawled into bed with him. Math had thought that she would sleep in one of the many other small beds in the room, but she snuggled in with him, pressing her body into his.

But by 5:00 am, she was already gone. Math checked his phone one more time—yes, it was really 5:00 am.

There were voices talking downstairs, and every once in a while, he heard someone walking down the hallway outside the room. It was barely light out as Math pulled on jeans and a T-shirt and went downstairs to find Tess.

Half a dozen eyes greeted him as he walked through the living room into the kitchen. Tasha was pouring a mug of coffee with a toddler on her hip when he walked in. The table had seven half-grown kids around it eating waffles. Tess wasn't around.

"Morning." He tried not to sound as exhausted as he felt.

"Morning, Mathias. Tess is outside if you are looking for her. She didn't think you would be up early." She poured him a cup of coffee with a smile as if she had gotten a full night of sleep.

"I didn't think she would be up so early either." He took it from her, nodding thanks.

"Tess doesn't get much sleep around here."

"Are these all yours?" He waved at all the kids.

"No, I have three of Ilya's. She went early to the hospital to be with Grandma, and Mike has to work this morning so can't be at the hospital," Tasha said.

"Did Tess go with her?" he asked.

"No, she is helping AJ with the morning chores. She usually does that. Tessa, do you want to take Mathias out to find Tess? I think he is missing her." She laughed as the teenager at the table got up.

"Sure, Mama, this way." He followed the girl out of the house. She looked a lot like her father, like Tess. He wondered if the baby Tess was carrying would look like this. Or would it look like all his other kids?

"So, you are named after Tess?"

She smiled. "I am named after everyone. When you don't know someone's name in this family, call them Terezilya, and you will probably be right."

"I will keep that in mind. So, have you lived your entire life?" He asked as he looked at the run-down farm. The house and barn both needed paint, and the garage was falling down.

"No, we have only been here about five years. Once Mom had the last two, and Mike and Terezilya's youngest mostly moved on, we got this place. I think that Mom and Dad will move when I go to college in three years. Then they will only have six at home again, and someone with a bigger family will get the big house." Math looked back at the house she considered big. His parents' house was bigger than it, and it was just the two of them in there.

"You just get moved when your family size changes?"

"Yup, except Ilya since they own their home. Her husband Peter bought it before they got married," Tessa said, then turned toward a grove of trees on the edge of the property. "That's where Tess's mom and dad live."

"Always?" he asked, looking at the small old trailer house in need of some repairs.

"No, they used to live with the boys, moving around a lot. But Tess used to either live with Ilya or Mom's parents. She didn't like moving and put her foot down at some point." Tessa chuckled.

Math opened the barn door as they got there and heard Tess talking somewhere inside, her voice carrying from the depths of the barn. At the sound, he told the teenager, "I can find her from here."

Walking into the barn, he saw her at the end, looking over the fence at pigs on the other side. A teenage boy was looking at the pigs as well and pointing at some. He was probably telling Tess the names of the pigs.

Today Tess was dressed in blue jeans and a gray sweatshirt that had seen way too many washings, with mud boots on her feet. Math smiled at the sight of her being relaxed in an old barn, looking at pigs. Miss Bank President in hog poop.

She turned around when she realized he was there. "Morning, Mathias."

"Morning, Tess, you're up early," he said as the boy left them alone.

"I do not get a lot of time here, so I do not waste it sleeping," she admitted.

"You should come more often." He walked toward her.

She gave him her typical excuse. "It is a long drive."

"I know, I just drove it." He grabbed the fence on either side of her and kissed her upturned mouth. Had he even gotten to kiss her yesterday? No, he couldn't remember kissing her at all. He hoped to make up for that today.

Raising his lips, he whispered, "I think you have been lying to me about what your name is. Say it like your family would say it."

With a half-grin, she replied, "Terezilya Aleksandrina Zsophia Aleksandrov."

"I am probably going to have to have you spell it one day." He grinned back and kissed her nose.

"You will be even more confused if you have the spelling."

He ran a hand over her still flat stomach. "How are you feeling today?"

"Good. I am happy I am here. Papa has surgery at 9:00 am, so I want to go to town for that." Her eyes dropped to watch his hand.

"I'm glad you let me bring you, though I wish you had asked." He leaned in and brushed a kiss across her forehead.

"Really? Were you not paying attention to the fight that happened in my office? No way was I bringing that man here. And I would have been fine on my own; I make this trip often enough." She reminded him of his biggest mistake.

It was hard to believe it was only yesterday morning that that had happened. So much had taken place it felt like weeks ago.

"Sorry about that fight. I panicked because I thought I was losing you, and I had just realized how much I wanted you." He apologized, and probably not for the last time about it.

"I was not leaving. I will stay for the baby," she argued as she crossed her arms.

Her words stopped him. "I want you to stay because *you* want to."

"I might not be what you want … once you get to know me." Her eyes went to her feet at the admission.

"I'm afraid only the opposite will be happening. I think I will be even more in love with you when we leave here than when we got here." He kissed her again, deeper this time.

Her arms had gone around him, and he leaned closer because he needed to feel more of her than he was. He had missed waking up next to her that morning.

Pushing him away, she smiled, "Stop, you will give the pigs ideas."

"Maybe we should have gotten a hotel."

"Now you back me up on that." She complained.

He followed her back to the house. "So, this is where you grew up?"

"No, I grew up near here. I can show you sometime while we are here, but this place is nicer than the others except for Ilya's house. I did not grow up rich like you. They are just as poor today as back then. Everyone works like dogs, and they still have nothing," Tess said as she opened the door for him and held it while he walked past her.

"They seem happy anyway," he whispered.

"There you two are! Now sit, and I will feed you," Tasha said from the now nearly empty kitchen with a wooden spoon in her hand. Only two kids remained at the table.

"You do not have to." Tess sat down when Tasha just gave her a look.

"So, Tasha, what is your husband doing this morning?" he asked.

"Alex?" she questioned as if she had another husband. "He is at the dairy barn until 8:00 am, and then he will be home."

"Is he on both shifts?" Tess asked.

"Yes, he is working as many shifts as he can. We want to buy a farm one day. We know now is not the time to be saving with all the kids at home, but we have to try."

Math fully expected Tess to have input, but she was strangely silent on her best friend's plan. He wondered if her financial advice wasn't accepted here. Instead, she just chewed her waffle and looked out the window. Maybe it was because her friend wasn't asking for a loan from her.

"Good luck," Math said, hoping Tasha would feel it was from both of them. Oddly, Tasha didn't even notice that Tess wasn't paying attention. She just went on making waffles.

By 8:30 am, Tess was changed into different blue jeans and a different sweatshirt borrowed from her sister since she hadn't brought a thing with her. In fact, nobody seemed to even notice it was odd. But then again, maybe she did this often.

Though she was dressed the same as her sister when they arrived at the hospital, Tess carried herself differently than the others. It seemed news had made it around the entire family of his being there; they all knew who he was: Tess's man.

Everyone that came to the hospital was friendly, and nobody actually spoke Russian to him just to test him. They all spoke English around him and only seemed to tease Tess in Russian when he was around, and that was only to make her mad or blush or both.

Her brothers all seemed to come in at about the same time, and he talked to them about farming. They were very interested in what farming was like in North Dakota. He asked them about farming here all their lives. Most of them had worked as farm labor since they got to this country in their late teens.

None of them had managed to scrape enough money together to buy land; it was just too high of a price for them with their large families. After talking to Alex, he had learned that the farm he had been so desperate to buy a few months before was cheap compared to what he was interested in buying. And he knew the man would never get enough money together for a down payment, no matter how many shifts he did at the dairy barn. Which might be why Tess had been silent that morning.

But mostly, he learned more about Tess. Most of the family called her Terezilya to her face, but when talking about her, they all called her Tess, mostly to distinguish her from all the other Terezilyas in the family. She had never noticed it. He had even met the sister-in-law with the same name, who Tess hated, but had given her a big hug since she was Tasha's mother.

As Math watched Tess talk with everyone, he was surprised to learn she knew what was happening in everyone's life, even living nine hours away. And they all hugged her upon seeing her and asked about the baby—they all knew. No one seemed to care that Tess was unmarried or that they didn't know Math at all. They were all just happy for Tess.

To his surprise, they had told him about all the jobs Tess had while in high school. From farm labor to raising animals to sell for a profit. Alex even talked about the summer he and she had spent with Tess working at the dairy farm, milking cows twice a day. Then they would bale hay between milking. It was exactly like he had made her move weeks before, all so Alex could buy a wedding ring for Tasha, and she could pay for her senior year in high school.

Whenever one of the women came in with a baby, they always seemed to end up with Tess, who would carry it around until either the mother left or the baby fell asleep. Math didn't know if they were doing it because Tess was pregnant or because Tess always did it. She didn't seem to notice that it was happening.

By the time the surgery was done, he had lost track of everyone who had come and gone. He did know they were gathering at Ilya's place since the hospital was too small for the entire family, but he was sure Ilya's place was too small as well. So far, Tess had stayed in hopes of seeing her father. She'd already anticipated returning to Landstad as soon as she could.

Leaning back in his chair, he watched her. She was exhausted but would never admit it and would probably be mad if he pointed it out in front of her family. That made him smile. He was starting to see why she didn't admit weakness. She must have noticed he was watching her because she turned to him and smiled back.

Walking his way, she said, "You must be bored here after so many hours. Did you want to go back to Tasha and Alex's?"

Taking her hand when she was near enough, he pulled her onto his lap, "No, I'm learning everything there is to know about you."

It surprised him when she went willingly. Her body settled into his as she rested her head on his shoulder and said quietly, "I cannot imagine there was anything interesting to learn about me."

Encircling her with his arms, he admitted, "I don't think I knew anything about you before we came here."

He felt her sigh and start to pull away from him. "I understand."

Math just held tight to her and replied, "I don't think you do, Tess. I think that you are waiting for me to run away from here as fast as I can. But really, I see the real you, the one few get to enjoy. And I'm enjoying her as well."

"I am always me," she argued.

"Nope, but you are going to be. I want Terezilya *and* the bank president. I want them both."

"I don't know what you are talking about, Mathias." She finally pushed out of his arms, and he let her go since her sister was looking at them. So far, he hadn't won over the older version of Tess, not like he had won over her mom. But her mom had been a marshmallow compared to her oldest daughter.

"This is who she is, under it all. You cannot change her." Ilya had walked up on him while he watched Tess walk away.

"I don't want to change her; her life has made her who she is. I like who she is."

"Why?" Ilya demanded in her thick accent.

"She is different." He used the word that everyone used for her, a word that said everything and nothing at the same time.

"She's been that way ever since she was a baby. When she was four and dying, I promised that I would let her be whatever she wanted to be if she lived. When she lived, I kept that promise. I helped her when I could: get into that school and found her jobs that paid well. Because she was different and was not going to be happy here. Will she be happy with you?" Ilya demanded, her eyes searching his for the truth.

"I hope so. I want her to be who she is," he admitted as he watched her talk to her mom.

"Good, she needs to be happy." Ilya smiled for the first time at him.

"What was she dying of?" he asked. She had just glossed over the statement, though it had made Math's blood run cold that she had ever been in danger.

"Starvation, she still eats little. You have to make sure she eats," Ilya stated.

He knew she had still been in Russia when it happened, that it had affected her even today. He knew it was the reason she sends money to those that need it, so they don't feel the hunger she has felt in her life.

Before long, the entire group left heading to Ilya's place to eat. The small house was full of people and food, some he had never seen and some he saw at every family event he had attended. As Math followed Tess through the line, he tried to take everything she took so that he could try it. But some things, he wasn't brave enough to try. Finding a place to eat was tricky, so they sat under a tree with her leaning into him.

As they ate, she told him what they were eating, and what things he hadn't taken, she let him try. When their plates were empty, Ilya brought out desserts to them. He now saw it as an effort to get her sister to eat more. And this time, it worked.

Tess might think no one would notice if she stopped coming here, but he could tell she was missed when she was gone. There was no way her family would let her just drift away without a fight.

CHAPTER 29

MATHIAS HAD CONVINCED her to stay until Monday morning, giving her one more day with her family. Tess had been ready to leave Sunday afternoon, but he wouldn't hear of it. He insisted that she needed to spend time with her family and not think about the bank for a day. As far as Tess could tell, everyone spoke to him in English at all times—except when they were trying to teach him new words.

After spending the morning in church with her entire family, Tess was sure that Mathias was never coming back. Though he had fallen asleep twice, he swore it was interesting. But there had been no translation for him for the three hours it had lasted, except when Tess would lean over and tell him this or that. Looking around, Tess was starting to think that most of her family didn't pay much attention to the service.

While Math had spent the afternoon with her brothers looking at fields and equipment, she had spent the day with Tasha and Ilya. Not that she was paying attention to what was going on around her, she was trying to decide whether Mathias had been completely scared off.

"What do you think, Tessy?" Tasha asked.

"I was not paying attention," Tess admitted to the group. It was best to be honest, after all.

"She is thinking about her man. He should be okay," Ilya said, tapping Tess's hand.

"I know he will be okay, Ilya. I am not thinking about him," she argued.

"What then?" Tasha turned her attention to her aunt.

"Nothing you should be concerned about." Tess shrugged off their concern.

"Is this about you not being Russian, Terezilya? Because you cannot stop being that. I think that your man likes you when you are Russian." Ilya winked at her.

Staring at her older sister, she wondered what that wink meant. What could she think Mathias likes about her being Russian? The older sister tapped her hand again and laughed.

"When the baby comes, I cannot come as often. It is a long drive for a child." Tess put the blame on the baby; no way could they yell at the baby.

"The baby will get used to it. You can bring his kids, too. They will like it here. Everyone likes it here," Tasha stated as if they had visitors constantly. Or ever.

"Mathias probably will not come back again," Tess said. No matter what he claimed, she knew the truth.

"The Mathias you brought with you or the Mathias that lives in your head? Because I think the one that you brought is coming back every time you do, especially when you have his baby," Ilya replied, pointing at the door the men had left through almost an hour before.

"You do not understand, Ilya. Mathias and I do not always get along. He just found out about the baby before we left, and he was not happy. He had to marry his first wife because she was pregnant, so he is not happy about the baby." Tess looked at the group. She hadn't wanted to tell them, but they had to stop thinking of her and Mathias as a couple. She, herself, had to stop thinking of them as a couple.

"Maybe if you hadn't been hiding her from him, he wouldn't have been upset," Tasha pointed out.

"I was not hiding her from him. I had told Mama, and then I was going to tell him. And it's your fault I had a bad day before that." She argued.

"You were the one questioning it, Tessy. You were the one thinking everyone was against you. *You*." Tasha insisted.

"You said I did not belong here." Tess reminded her.

"You don't. You have always been different, Terezilya, always. You have made a place for yourself out there. You could never be happy back here because you weren't happy here before," Ilya replied as she pushed a plate of cookies toward her.

"I had a very happy childhood, Ilya," Tess said flatly. She wouldn't have traded it for anything.

"Of course, you did. But once you realized there was something else out there, you were gone. Private school and college. You worked your tail off to get away from here and you succeeded," Tasha pointed out.

"So?" Tess demanded.

"So, nothing. You have dreams the rest of us do not have. We are happy to be here; you want to leave. Even now, you are ready to go back. Mathias told you that you had to stay until tomorrow. You would have been gone already," Tasha said.

"I have a job, Tasha. I need to be at my job," Tess reminded her niece, frowning.

"And I know you get days off from your job. And on those days off, you have to come here with your baby and your family."

"I don't have a family," Tess corrected. Did she have to remind them again that she and Mathias were not a couple?

"You will. He has kids already. They will come next time," Ilya said, nodding.

"We are not a couple."

"You are having a baby." Ilya didn't need to remind her; it was something she couldn't very well forget.

"We just had sex, Ilya," Tess said.

"He came with you here. And so far, he has not run away."

"My car is broken," Tess stated, crossing her arms.

"You still brought him because you love him," Tasha said and tapped at Tess's chest, where her heart was.

"I do not," Tess hissed at her niece.

"Oh, yes you do, Terezilya. I know you, and you are in love." Ilya pointed to her.

"I beg to argue with you on this!" Tess stood up to leave. She couldn't talk to these people.

"Argue away, but you have been head over heels for that man for months," Tasha stated.

"I have not. I could barely stand him for months." Tess glared at her niece.

"He didn't like you, Terezilya, but you always liked him from day one."

Sadly, her sister was right. Tess had thought the man was gorgeous ever since he'd first walked into her bank. Mostly she had tried to stay away from him because she didn't want to stay in Landstad, but he had changed that for her. It was now where she belonged and wanted to be.

Pushing away from the table, she left her family. At this point, she didn't care what they were thinking; she needed time to think for herself. Heading out of the house, she went straight to the barn, where the animals were.

Tess leaned against the gate and looked at the black and white creatures who were milling around the pasture beyond. They paid no attention to her, and she barely noticed them.

When had she let herself fall for Mathias? Because Ilya was right—she was in love with the man and had been for a long time. But her feelings for him didn't matter. He went from hot to cold about her every few days. When he was hot it was easy to forget that they were over when they had left Landstad and that he didn't even want the baby she carried. She was a fool for him.

Since he had gotten her out of her car, he had been the Mathias that she was deeply in love with, but the other Mathias was still there in him. Now he knew of her past, where she came from. Tess was certain that bringing him to meet her family was just going to be another one of her big mistakes. Her personal life had never turned out as well as her professional one did.

"I found you," Mathias said softly, pulling her from her thoughts.

"I did not know I was lost." She glanced sideways at him leaning on the fence with her.

"Not lost, but not where I left you." He looked at the cows in the pen as well. "I could have sworn you once told me that you know nothing about cows."

"I said I did not know anything about *beef* cows. These are dairy," she pointed out as Math smiled. "What would you have done that day if I had told you I was raised on a farm?"

Could everything have been different if she had just admitted the truth? Would they have had more time together? Would they still have fought often?

Pulling her into his arms, he replied, "I don't know, but what I should have done was ask you to marry me on the spot."

"You did not even know me. Plus, you hated me."

"I tried to hate you, I really did. But I also really wanted to kiss you again and again." He did kiss her then.

Pulling back from him, she said, "No, you did not. You still hated me days later."

"I was an idiot. I should have demanded you marry me instead of going to Dottie's to eat Easter ham." He pulled her back.

"Demanded?" She raised an eyebrow at him in question.

"Demanded, Tess. Now, will you marry me? We have a kid coming." He ran a hand over her stomach, over their growing baby.

"No, Mathias. I will not marry you because of the baby," she insisted. She wasn't going to be another forced marriage for him to regret.

"Marry me because I love you too much to let you go." He pulled her closer to him as if to prove he couldn't let her go.

"No, I cannot marry you. You still hate me."

With knitted brows, he shook his head. "I don't hate you. But I admit I don't understand you sometimes. But now I have seen you here."

"I am no different from when you came into my office for a loan, Mathias," she assured him, knowing that any talk of that loan set him off. But right now, she was buckling under the pressure, and him storming off would release it.

His words made her want to say yes and jump into his arms, but she couldn't. Not yet. It had only been a few days ago that he had rejected not only her but the baby she carried. They had things to work out before she could let herself give in to him completely.

"You might not be, but I am. All I saw that day was a cool, confident woman that had a set of nice breasts. Have I ever told you how much I have always liked those?" He looked down at them. How he thought that she could miss his constant attention to that part of her body, she didn't know.

"But not someone you liked," she reminded him.

"But every time I saw you, every time I got to know you more, I liked you more and more. When I made you work on the farm, I wanted to see you run. I wanted to show myself that you didn't belong there, but everything you did proved again and again that I was completely wrong about you."

"The baby will love the farm; you do not have to worry about that." She looked away from him, not wanting to have him see how much she wanted to be there too. But not wanting to force his hand.

"Tess Thorn, I don't want the baby to love the farm. I don't care about the baby."

"O-okay," she stammered. *Now what? He didn't even want the baby anymore?*

"Wait, that didn't come out right. I want *you* there, Tess. Not just for the baby, though I really like the idea of you carrying our baby. Fuck, I love that you're carrying our baby, that we're having a baby together." He grabbed her and spun her around, pressing her to the fence. "We are going to name her after you."

"Mathias, stop." She laughed at his antics and pushed at his shoulders.

He started kissing her neck. "Not until you say you will move in with me."

"It is too soon." Her fingers curled into his shirt, unable to push him away like always.

"Too soon? We only have six months to prepare for our princess, woman, and I can't sleep without you anymore. I need you there. Plus, your brothers have been teaching me Russian, so I can understand you when you come." He cupped her butt and lifted her off the ground, still pressing her to the fence but rubbing her with his erection enough to make her hot.

"You are acting crazy. Put me down," she said but didn't mean it. This is where she wanted to be forever, in Mathias's arms, with the smell of nature surrounding them.

"I am crazy in love with you. Tell me you at least like me a little." His eyes looked into hers.

Cupping his face and running her thumbs over his lips, she whispered, "Yes, Mathias, I love you. Oh, so much."

"This time in Russian," he whispered, and when she said it, he groaned, "Marry me, Tess Thorn from the bank, and say those words to me every day until I die."

"No, it is too soon for marriage. We barely get along sometimes." She nipped at his neck, inhaling the smell that was all him.

"I should have asked you when I asked for the loan." He shifted so his hands could slip under her borrowed sweatshirt.

"I would have said no, just like with the loan." She giggled as his fingers ran over her ribs.

"No, you would have said it was too soon, but then now you would have been ready." He kissed her lips. "But you are as stubborn as your mama, so I will have to wear you down."

"Wear away, Mathias, wear away."

EPILOGUE

THE CHURCH WAS STIFLING HOT, and Tess was sure she was going to pass out at any moment. Math wasn't helping at all by insisting that he hold her hand and press his leg into hers. It was like the heat didn't affect him at all. But maybe it didn't because he wasn't pregnant!

"We should get married here," Math said ever so casually. It was what he said nearly every Sunday when they attended church since getting back from New Paris.

"I prefer my church." She shifted away from him and his intense heat.

He perked up and scooted back into her. "So, you will marry me finally?"

"I didn't say that. I just said that I prefer to get married in my church. When I get married to whoever I marry," she said, knowing that it would get a rise out of the man. It had been a few months of her turning him down, but she wasn't going to rush into marriage just because she was pregnant. After all, her entire family already knew, not to mention the entire town around them. There was no way to put that genie back in the bottle.

Tess was sure it was Mia who had made the gossip spread, becoming old news by the time she and Math returned to Landstad.

Mia only had a few details, but she had been able to seamlessly fill in any blank there was.

Math had called his kids and broke the news before the gossip could get to them. Cora was upset because she didn't want to have to raise a baby—as if she would have to. Mason didn't care, and Juniper was more excited than Math's mom was about it. Tess was sure the older woman was now going to pressure her daughters about having more kids. Or pressure them more than usual.

Over the past few months, there were some things that she gave in on easily: moving in with him, getting a new vehicle, speaking Russian more often. Since her brothers had taught Math a few words, he liked to use them when he could. Not that he said them even close to correctly, but he was trying, so it counted.

Not once since they drove back into town had she stayed at her apartment. In fact, she had moved out already. There was no way Math would let her not stay in their bed at night. He and Hue had cleaned out her place one day when she was working. It should have made her mad, but it hadn't. But he had done it right before the first of the month, so she didn't have to pay another month's rent. She wasn't cheap, but she did like to save money when she could.

"Stubborn like your mama, you are," Math grumbled and turned to his dad to say something about the wheat crop. He was getting used to the rejection.

The biggest change since she'd started dating Math was at the bank. It seemed that dating a local had been her ticket to work friend-ships. Every day, someone asked her about Math or the kids or the farm, or even the baby. The tellers were even planning a little baby shower one day. Suddenly, she was included in conversations that used to take place behind her back. The instant change of attitude had been unnerving at first; she had a feeling something was up. Math had sworn to her that the bank employees were not that deviant, but she had her doubts.

"Shot him down again?" Mandy asked from beside her. In the pew, Tess could feel her giggle.

"He's not serious most of the time," Tess told her, and it was true. It had turned into more of a joke between them than real. One day it would be real, and she would know it.

"Real or not, I think he is willing to take a yes at any moment," Mandy assured her.

"And one day, I will say yes, just not at Natalie's wedding. How rude is that?"

"Rude is making us sit in this heat for an extra ten minutes. It was supposed to start already," Mandy said and looked at the door at the back of the church.

"Do you think Mia lost control of the wedding?" Tess asked. Mia was the personal attendant to the bride, and she was in charge of almost everything and everyone during the wedding.

"After all the partying the groom did last night, maybe he is still sobering up? Or at least that's what I heard." Mandy looked around the church again as if anything had changed in the last few minutes.

Tess followed her gaze and saw Ruth and Anderson sitting a few pews behind them. Anderson had his arm around his girlfriend's shoulders even in the heat. It was nice to see her happy.

The only other book club member was in the back of the church with her son, a boy who didn't seem all that interested in being there. Hazel was trying to keep him occupied, but she seemed as interested as Tess was about getting out of the hot church.

Two days ago, Tess had seen the extent of Hazel's reaction to Natalie. For months they had been cordial, and Tess didn't understand why they weren't closer. After seeing the woman's panic attack, she now knew exactly why. Amanda had given her a brief overview of the accident that took the lives of Hazel's brother and sister, an accident that Natalie was involved in.

Tess's heart went out to the younger members of the group. Even if Natalie was getting married, she didn't seem all that happy about it. But then again, maybe that was because she was moving away, and like Tess, she saw that this town might be home.

Another wave of heat washed over Tess, and she shifted away from Math, only to get too close to Mandy. She was trapped between two hot Nordskov's and couldn't get away from them. Most of the time, she didn't want to, but today, right now, she needed some space.

"I am going to the ladies' room," she said to Math.

"The wedding is about to start. Can it wait?"

"No, it cannot. I have a tiny human sitting on my bladder," she said, though it wasn't true. She just needed out.

"Are you feeling okay?" Mandy asked from beside her, more concerned than she needed to be.

"Fine. I just have to pee," she said as quietly as she could since the people around them were starting to pay attention to them.

She heard someone behind her, probably Mia's mom, announce too loudly that Tess was feeling sick. There were more murmurs from those with the woman, who must be Mia's sisters.

Turning to them, she stated, "I am fine."

"You look pale, dear," Dotty said and patted her shoulder. "Math, you need to take better care of your—" she paused for a moment "—girlfriend."

"Fiancé, Aunt Dotty. She just hasn't said yes yet," Math told his aunt through gritted teeth.

"She has to say yes before you can call her your fiancé," Mandy argued with her brother,

"Stop, stop, I am fine, everyone. I will wait until after the wedding." She wasn't moving now. Everyone was looking!

"Math, just take her home. She'll feel better at home," Dolly said from down the pew, nearly yelling.

"I am staying for the wedding!" she told her future mother-in-law. After all, she wasn't that far along that it was excusable to not attend functions because she was pregnant.

"Everyone would understand." Dotty patted her shoulder again. "When I was pregnant with Mia, I was so sick I couldn't leave the farm. I swore I would never have another baby."

"Yet you still went on to have five more," Dolly said.

"Mia seemed lonely all by herself. The rest were a breeze," Dotty told her sister.

Tess let the sisters talk about pregnancies and babies, happy that nobody was talking to her or about her anymore. Landstad was just as bad as her family, always gossiping about someone and something. It usually made her comfortable, but not today. Not in this heat.

Sitting back, she stared at the front of the church. She had been excited about this wedding; she hadn't been to any weddings besides family weddings. This would be the first one to show her how others were. Tess was sure she would give in and get married here. All their friends were there, as well as his entire family. Her family would understand.

Once she was ready to marry Math, she would pretend to give in and marry him right here. Just not on the hottest day of the year—maybe the coldest, like her birthday. That had turned out better than expected.

Despite the heat, she took his hand and squeezed it. At the movement, he turned to her, and she met his eyes. Who would have thought six months later, they would be sitting side-by-side in a church of all places? In love and planning the arrival of their daughter.

It wasn't that long ago that she was sure she would never make a new friend again, but here she was with friends, and soon, she'd have a new family. All because she dared to answer a post about a serial killer.

Under her leg, her phone buzzed once with an incoming message. Pulling it out with her free hand, she looked at the screen. Beside her, Mandy was looking at her own phone. They looked at each other and got to their feet in the same instant. They had gotten the same message.

Mia: Basement, now!!!

EPILOGUE

Bonus Epilogue

OF COURSE, Mathias won in the end. He seemed to always get his way with her. Not that she was complaining about it, except when she did. It was annoying that he would get his way *all* the time.

Tess sat quietly on their bed, the one that they had shared since he took her home from New Paris. Not once had he willingly let her sleep apart from him. On rare occasions, she had done it, but he would pout about it and complain. But then he would show her how much she was missed, and she forgave him.

Tonight was one of those rare nights she would not share his bed, and he had been crabby all day. Not that she cared too much about his anger at her. That had dissipated with time, and she let him have his moods. In the end, he was the man she loved. All of him.

As she shifted the baby to her other breast, Math walked into the room and grinned at her, his eyes not on hers. He still liked her breasts, and he was usually looking at them even after seeing them time and time again.

Though pregnancy had affected them as well as the rest of her,

Math still seemed to love every part of her. From the extra pounds to the stretch marks, he had made sure to cherish her every day they had together.

She purposefully left her breast exposed as she watched him walk across the room toward her. He didn't miss the opportunity to see her. Looking at him never got old for her, either. He was still as good-looking as when he had sat in her bank over a year before.

"Tell her that Daddy loves her." He sat near them and ran his hand over the white-blonde hair of his youngest.

Tess did in Russian and watched Mathias's eyes grow dark with desire. After they had returned from her family, she had started to speak it more often, in passion and in anger. Now she tried to instill the language in their baby girl. Maybe she would never be fluent in it, but she would have some knowledge of it. That would be enough.

"Mathias Nordskov, stop that," she warned over the baby's head.

"What?" His hand slid from the baby's head and over to her exposed breast.

"I cannot have you getting bedroom eyes when I speak to our child." She couldn't push his hand away because she was holding the baby with both of hers.

"Bedroom eyes?" He grinned at her and realized she was trapped as his fingers pebbled the nipple that had just fed their daughter.

"*Mathias*," she warned again, but not as forcefully.

"I can't help that you are incredibly sexy right now. Or that you are talking so sexy. I love when you speak all sexy," he said.

Over the months they'd been together, she had tried not to think about what he had been like with Karen and her pregnancies. Had he been as attentive? Had he been nervous when it wasn't his fourth child? Did he compare them?

He rarely said anything unless it was something new to him, like breastfeeding. Karen had been against it and had never even tried. So, Tess got to be the one that taught him about it, including getting to watch him marvel over them whenever he walked in when she was feeding the baby.

"We agreed that the baby should be raised bilingual, and that means that you cannot think about sex every time I speak Russian to her." They hadn't actually discussed it. Mathias had just said it, and Tess hadn't argued with him. It had been more of an announcement than anything else.

"I wouldn't if her mama wasn't so sexy when she spoke it." Mathias unbuttoned the remaining buttons of her shirt.

"Mathias, the children," she stated since they were all in the house today. They had accepted her willingly and happily from the beginning. Even Cora had been happy that her dad was happy.

She loved the kids, though she did like that Karen took the older kids every other weekend and some days during the week, giving her and Mathias time alone. Sometimes, she just liked to be alone with her man, though that had gotten harder when the baby finally came.

"My mom just picked them up for the afternoon, so we're alone." Whispering, he pushed her shirt off her shoulder, then his lips caressed the newly exposed skin.

"I am feeding this one." She nodded at her.

"She's almost done, and she's sleeping." Lifting his head, he ran a hand over his daughter. Tess loved how much he loved their daughter. All her worries that he wouldn't want the baby were for nothing. He still swore he couldn't think straight after she told him. Something he regrets still.

It seemed that while she was away with her papa, word had leaked throughout the book club and then throughout town that she was pregnant and by who. All thanks to Mia, so that by the time she got back, gossip had moved on. Except for Mathias's mother, who demanded to be told first next time.

Mathias took the baby from her arms and carried her to her room across the hallway. It had taken a bit of shifting to get the four kids settled into the little house, but Mathias had been happy to give up his office for Juniper so that the new baby could sleep near her parents.

Back in the room, Mathias shed his shirt and pants as he climbed into bed with her. "Oh, is that how it is going to be?"

"Yes, it is. I have missed you all day." He nuzzled her neck.

"Wait one moment, Mathias. I am still mad at you. You cannot always get your way all the time." She pushed him away from her.

"What have I ever gotten my way on?" He let himself fall onto the bed and crossed his arms.

"One, I moved in here, and you cleaned out my apartment without me. You and Hue," she said, pulling her shirt closed.

"You said you didn't care. You were working, and you wanted to live here with me. Right where I wanted you. It was a win-win." He rolled back toward her with a smile.

"Two, you named the baby after me after I said no." He had fought for the name for weeks, and in the end, she relented. It was, after all, her mother's name.

"I named her after Tasha's mother, and you know that. I know she and you have some history, but the woman loves me, and I wanted to name my baby after her." He pulled her down and rolled on top of her. "It isn't my fault you share her name, Terezilya."

The way he said it was still slightly wrong, but it might have been his North Dakota accent and not his ability to say the name. It still didn't roll off his tongue, but he was trying. And even though he could say it, he only called her that name when he thought she needed a reminder of who she was: a country girl.

Although they had saddled their daughter with a long name, her nickname Zia was far more fitting to the tiny baby. And Tess loved it.

"You are super annoying." She giggled.

"Sadly, you love me and have to put up with me until I have completely worn you down." He nuzzled her neck as he opened her shirt and slipped his hands over her breasts.

Gasping, she threw up her hands and said, "Consider me worn. Marry me, Mathias Nordskov."

He went perfectly still in her arms.

Maybe he wasn't ready yet. Maybe his asking all the time was just a habit now, and he didn't want to marry her anymore. Did he not want to marry her anymore? Had it all been for the baby, and now it didn't seem important to him anymore?

Rolling off her, he grabbed his phone from beside the bed and started to type. Watching him, she wondered who he suddenly needed to send a message to. Why wouldn't he just answer her?

Beside her, her phone sounded the familiar ping of a text. Grabbing it, she looked at the message she had received.

Tasha: He said yes.

"Did you text my niece your answer?" She looked over at him, bewildered.

"Yes. She would be the first you texted, so now I can make love with my fiancé and not have to worry about being interrupted with texts." He pulled her on top of him as her phone started to make noises.

She giggled. "You thought Tasha could keep her mouth shut?"

"I thought the distance would be enough." He peeled off her shirt with a grin.

She laughed at Math. Her niece now lived down the road from them, but one mile or nine hours didn't change how fast she was in contact with everyone else. Over the winter, Tasha and Alex had moved with their kids here to North Dakota. The couple had been able to purchase the farm and land that Math had been looking at the day they met. To Tess's delight, Tasha was watching the baby for her, and Alex was working for Math as he started his farm.

Her phone was still announcing more texts as Mathias slid her pants over her hips. "I think next time you should wait to tell people. At least until morning."

"Stop talking, Mathias." She worked at getting the rest of her clothes off. "We only have minutes before the family descends on us. And I want to make love to you."

He watched her and touched her as she pulled off her leggings and panties in one go. As always with Mathias, she was wet and hot as she straddled his hips, and she knew she had slipped into Russian when she repeated, "minutes."

"All I need is minutes, future Mrs. Nordskov. There is no way…" His voice trailed off as she slid down his hard cock.

The sex was hot, loud, and fast, and by the time Tasha and Alex drove into the yard, the engaged couple was dressed and all smiles, happy to celebrate with friends. Though she was sure Mathias had never dreamed a text could start a party.

Even when his parents and kids came over, along with anyone else Tasha had a phone number for, he seemed surprised. But not Tess; this was normal. This was exactly how good news was celebrated back home.

Landstad was the home she had been looking for since she'd left her parents' house. Or, more importantly, Mathias Nordskov was that home, and his community had accepted her for who she was.

She had finally found the home she always craved—in a little town in North Dakota with a farmer.

THE END

Thank you so much for reading Invisible. Did you love it? Reviews mean everything to indie writers – you can leave a review for Invisible on Amazon!

Book Club member Natalie Beckett falls for her former history teacher after running from her own wedding in Impulsive.

ALSO BY ALIE GARNETT

Landstad, ND

Invisible

Irresistible

Impulsive

Insuppressible

Intriguing

Imperfect

Irreplaceable

The Great Lovely Falls

Falling for the Single Mom

Falling for his Best Friends Sister

Falling for the Boss

Falling for his Step-Sister

Falling for his Fake Wife

Falling into a Second Chance

Hart Series

Seeing her Pain

Her Favor

Max Valentine is Looking at Me!

Keeping her Safe

Stand Alone

Romancing the Doctor

ABOUT THE AUTHOR

Alie Garnett loves a little spice in her books. She lives on a small hobby farm in northern Minnesota with her husband and two kids. When she isn't writing, she is doing everything that she didn't 'get to' while writing.